SACRAMENTO PUBLIC LIBRARY
828 "I" Street
Sacramento, CA 95814
11/16

I0764699

CRISTINA SÁNCHEZ-ANDRADE

THE WINTERLINGS

Translated from the Spanish
by Samuel Rutter

RESTLESS BOOKS
BROOKLYN, NEW YORK

Copyright © 2014, 2016 Cristina Sánchez-Andrade
Translation copyright © 2016 Samuel Rutter

First published as *Las Inviernas* by Anagrama, Barcelona, 2014

All rights reserved. No part of this book may be reproduced or
transmitted without the prior written permission of the
publisher.

First Restless Books paperback edition November 2016

ISBN: 978-1-63206-109-6
Library of Congress Control Number: 2016940771

Cover design by Rodrigo Corral
Typeset by Tetragon, London

Ellison, Stavans, and Hochstein LP
232 3rd Street, Suite A111
Brooklyn, NY 11215

www.restlessbooks.com
publisher@restlessbooks.com

For my grandmother Isidora,
who gifted us all these stories.

PART I

This cold isn't yours.
It's an empty cold forgotten by no one knows who . . . .
Silence. The snow of another story is slipping through your fingers.

OLGA OROZCO,
"I ROW AGAINST THE NIGHT"
(TRANS. MARY CROW)

THEY CAME PAST one morning like the thrumming of a hornet, swifter than an instant.

The women.

The Winterlings.

The men bent over the earth straightened up to watch. The women stilled their brooms. The children stopped playing; two women with big, tired bones, as though worn down by life, were crossing the town square.

Two women followed by four sheep and a cow with a swinging gait, pulling a covered wagon filled with provisions and utensils.

Still standing at the end of a path that zigzagged between clumps of turnip greens was their grandfather's old house—their house, too—covered now by the branches of a fig tree.

Bats and owls crashed into each other, flying in loops. Ivy had invaded the house, and the chimney, bursting with foliage, had acquired the dimensions and appearance of a crumbling tower. The house had an orchard with a lemon tree, and bushes that sheltered butterflies and rustling noises; out back, a river coursed with slender and succulent trout.

Beyond the river, the forest sprang up in thick trees. The greenery, taut and dense, wove itself together from the ground to the crowns of the trees, surrounded by vegetable gardens and tiny tilled plots.

It was raining, and they went inside.

The women and the animals.

They swept the floor. They pulled down the cobwebs. They put away the provisions they had brought. They made soup. The light dwindled, and the cold sharpened.

A domestic, familiar smell enveloped them; it reminded them of the sweetness of certain summer days, lunches in the orchard, and their lost childhood. But the smell also spoke to them of the war, of dampness, and of laughter. Of mice. Of anger.

One of the women sat down next to the other.

"We'll be fine," she said.

"Yes," came the reply.

They whiled away the time sipping at the soup, immersed in their conversation.

"We'll be fine."

It wasn't fear. Perhaps it was suspicion, a strange intuition.

"We will."

AWAY FROM TIERRA DE CHÁ, they had managed to adjust themselves to other climes and customs, but had never stopped dreaming of the house and the fig tree, of green meadows in the rain.

Apart from the fig tree that had grown twisted and sprawling across the roof, the house remained just as they had left it when they fled almost thirty years ago.

Now, sitting at the table, they took in everything with tears in their eyes, while the soup began to go cold.

And they remembered.

Coming into the house, on the left, after the cool hallway where the dogs always slumbered, was the kitchen that opened onto the orchard. The orchard would bloom extraordinarily in spring, with pear trees and apple trees, a lemon tree, bougainvillea with an exquisite aroma that filled the rooms, hydrangeas, a pigeon loft with no pigeons, a haystack, and flower beds.

When the pears fell, their booming could be heard from the back of the house, and the chickens would run about terrified.

In the house, there was neither running water nor a bathroom. They used some holes facing the stable as a lavatory, and covered them with gorse branches to camouflage the smell.

Then there was the attic. In the attic, they kept sewing machines, spools of thread, candles, trunks, books, papers, bed linen, and potatoes with thick purple sprouts.

In the attic, children used to cry, and there were dead birds, umbrellas with broken stretchers, spiderwebs, and bats.

They remembered that very clearly.

They remembered as well that animals and humans lived together inside the house. An altogether pleasant cohabitation—a smelly, uncomfortable mess that was tolerated to keep warm, the real purpose of which was to keep warm. The stable was very close to the kitchen, just below the bedrooms.

When night fell, both the lowing of the cows, and the men themselves, drifted up the stairs.

Well-lit by the fire that crackled in the hearth, the kitchen in that house had always been a place for the folks of Tierra de Chá to meet.

While corn was shucked, chestnuts roasted, or sweaters knitted, outlandish tales were told: a she-wolf that came into the village to carry off newborns; a snake that suckled gently from the udders of a cow; mythical stories of donkeys laden with saddlebags filled with gold . . . (Do you remember? Of course I remember, woman!)

By the hearth, they also spoke of Cuba. Many people from the village had immigrated there, mostly to avoid being sent to the war in Morocco as conscripts, and in Cuba there was money dangling from the trees, with gold coins and pearl necklaces instead of pears or apples. In Cuba, they ate parrot stew and stuffed hummingbird, and the women strolled naked through the streets.

Directly in front of the hearth sat Don Reinaldo, the Winterlings' grandfather. One of the wisest and most influential men in the village, he was dressed as always in corduroy, with his scraggy tobacco-stained beard and his eyes as blue as the sea. On winter nights, he would insist that there had always been many madmen in the village. Then he would tell the story of the man who came back from who knows where and declared himself a chicken. He was so deranged that he even laid eggs, and the family put up with his madness just so they wouldn't miss out on fresh eggs.

Don Manuel, the priest in Tierra de Chá, used to sit between the two Winterlings, who were only little girls back then. He was short and fat, an absolute glutton. He was always somewhere between dinner and Mass. As soon as he finished the sermon, he'd be out and into the street. With great strides, pulling up his cassock to keep the manure off it, he would cross the square to eat his lunch. While the maid was tying a napkin around his neck and serving him, he positively burbled with pleasure. His mouth watered at the sight of what lay before him: a hearty broth, complete with turnip greens, potatoes, and bacon, spicy sausage and ribs, then a couple of chops or some eggs fried in bacon fat, a hunk of bread, and half a liter of local wine. And for dessert, rice pudding made with butter that left the sticky traces of kisses from his mother on his palate. And he never skipped the brandy and the coffee.

No one ever wanted to sit next to him because he gave off a certain smell. It wasn't the smell of the stable, or of sweat, or even of cooking: the priest smelled of musty clothes and of priest. It was a brown-colored smell—in any case, a smell that was somehow linked with pious old ladies and steamed cauliflower.

Opposite him sat Mr. Tenderlove, a dental mechanic, as well as Uncle Rosendo, the country teacher. Then a bit further away from the fireplace, next to . . . What was his name again? asked one of the Winterlings. I can't remember, answered the other . . . Well, that fellow, the man who raised capons, and the women of course, few or many of them, depending on the day. (Tristán. The man who raised capons was called Tristán.) The one woman who was always there was Meis's Widow—ample of thigh and scarce of calf, with the

13

shadow of a moustache on her upper lip, like nearly all the women in Tierra de Chá. She would throw seductive glances over at Uncle Rosendo, seated at the other end, and he would respond by removing his cap and sighing.

Don Reinaldo's maid, who went by the name of Esperanza, also sat by the hearth with her son, Little Ramón.

Now they remembered, yes; Little Ramón, with a big head but tiny little ears like cherries, who liked to take the breast by the shelter of the hearth, in those warm and peaceful surroundings where the faint but pleasant odor of sausage and the smoke from gorse-bush roots were always in the air. (Do you remember? How could I not remember?) After siesta time, he would run off to fetch his stool and curl up near the women to listen to their stories.

Tierra de Chá was a very remote village, and its inhabitants were known to be very poor. But, as people used to say around those parts, they were also known to be very attached to their mothers.

One real mama's boy was Little Ramón. At the first little whimper, his mother would unbutton her blouse and wedge him up against her huge, veiny breasts, which tasted like curdled milk. The boy sucked the first nipple, then the second one, and his mouth was so full of breast that the milk dribbled out the corners of his mouth and ran down his neck. Only every now and again, when the boy bit on a nipple with his teeth, would that woman, sitting as still as a rock, give a little jump of surprise.

Oh, Ramón, Little Ramón; everyone knew who his mother was, but very few knew his father.

One day, the Winterlings' grandfather came in and sat by the hearth. When he saw the boy, who must have been at least six or seven, could already talk the hind legs off a horse, and could already read books by himself, he put his hands to his head in disbelief.

"Look, woman," he said to Esperanza. "That kid isn't a suckling anymore. You'll have to do something about it."

But the maid just shrugged. She said if it weren't for the nipple, the kid would never open his mouth. In reality, it was not because of poverty but because of her own pride that the kid carried on with his vice; she didn't want her son to have to bear the same cross that she had.

Her cross to bear had been the following: she was abandoned very young, and a poor woman by the name of Nicolasa had found her by the door of her house when she came home from the hot baths at Lugo. She had been wrapped up tightly and left in a basket with a bottle of sweet wine and some freshly prepared *filloa* pancakes. The woman picked up the basket and while she ate the pancakes she thought about a name for the girl. She came up with the name Esperanza a la Puerta de Nicolasa—Hope at Nicolasa's Door—and for years fed her with the milk of a nanny goat, letting her suckle directly from the animal. The goat grew fond of the girl, and each day, when she came down from the mountain, she'd rush ahead of the flock, nudging the door open with her muzzle, searching for the girl in the house and then raising a leg to offer her an udder.

For years in the village, they laughed about the girl suckled by a nanny goat, and as soon as Esperanza was old enough to think about it, she swore to herself that the first thing she'd give to her child would be the breast that was never given to her ("a breast like God intended," she used to say).

And so it had gone for seven years, until the day of the weaning, when Don Reinaldo brought it to her attention.

The Winterlings remembered how he had gone around the whole village that day, spouting his opinion. Mrs. Francisca, a baker and mother of eight children, put in her piece: "Give him mashed stew, woman."

Along came Aunty Esteba, who was in charge of dressing the deceased, and said, "He'll suck you dry."

Gumersinda, limping along, pointed with her finger and pronounced, "You'll have him hooked on there your whole life!"

The priest came and advised: "Pray—that always helps."

The mother of the child shrugged. To everyone she gave the same reply: "If it weren't for the nipple, the kid wouldn't open his mouth."

A few days later, the grandfather came back with a little bowl filled with an ointment he had prepared himself with bitter herbs, ash, and lemon juice.

"Tomorrow, smear this on your breasts," he ordered. "And you'll see, the kid will never suck a nipple again in his life."

The next morning, the woman smeared her breasts with the ointment. Soon enough, the kid came over with his stool and sat down to start suckling. He gave it three or four licks, but then he pushed the nipple away with a look of disgust.

"Well then, Little Ramón?" the women asked mockingly. "No tit today?"

Much later on, when Esperanza had died, and Little Ramón was just Ramón and had become a sailor, and had once disappeared on a ship for two whole years, he still gave the same response: "The tit's terrible today."

They remembered this, and many other things besides, while they set up the house again.

Tears falling into the soup.

The Winterlings.

3

NOW THEY SLEPT like they had as children: snoring with their mouths open in a bedroom with a wet and leaky roof, a window that looked out over the plots, a crucifix, a photo of Clark Gable, and two little iron beds with mattresses filled with corn husks. They slumped over the beds like prehistoric lizards. No one had bothered them since their arrival. Then early one morning, disturbed by a noise, one of them opened an eye suddenly.

"Hey, what was that?" she said to her sister.

And she stayed like that for a while, with one eye open and the other closed, her hands like paws over the turned-down covers, still and cold as a lizard.

The other Winterling, who had finally woken, got up straight away. Sitting on the bed, she strained her ears to listen.

"I can't hear anything . . . " she said.

"That's because you're still half asleep," answered the other.

"You make it your business to know everything," retorted the first one. She stretched out an arm and began to feel her way along the nightstand. "What would you know about my sleep? My sleep is mine, not yours. Where are my teeth? Did you take them?"

"And what would I want with your disgusting teeth?"

The one who had just spoken yawned, and the other one saw right into the roof of her mouth, which was red like the entrails of a pig.

"I don't know why you have to be so mean," said the first one. She kept feeling along the nightstand until she found her dentures. She popped them in with a hollow sound: *plop*. Then she jumped out of bed, pulled out the chamber pot from underneath it, and lifted up her nightdress. "Nobody in their right mind would put up with you," she continued, squatting to relieve herself. "You're lucky you've got me."

When she finished, her sister took her spot atop the chamber pot.

One of them standing, the other squatting, they strained to listen again.

"And what if it's the Civil Guard coming to get us? *They'll* surely come along some day . . . " said the one who was squatting. She stood up, adjusted her nightdress, and hid the chamber pot back under the bed.

"It's just Greta," said the other soothingly. "She's been driven mad by the horseflies." She went over to the trapdoor in the floor and pulled it up. Like the revelation of something hidden, the acrid and seeping stench of the gorse used as bedding by the animals in the stable floated up. There was the Galician Red cow, which instead of being called Marela, or Teixa, like all the other cows in Tierra de Chá, was called Greta. Greta Garbo. Once she saw the cow's rump encrusted with muck, and its tail switching back and forth to swat away the flies, the Winterling sighed calmly.

For a while she stayed like that, crouching, her head hanging down through the trapdoor. She listened to the creaking of her jawbone and whispered maternal words to the cow: "Don't you worry, Little Greta, here we are . . . " She would never use sweet little words like those with people, but she was sedated by the penetrating aroma that overcame her—overcame both of them—and went out through the door and spread through the forest, continuing on, on, into the north. It was a forest in which you could spend days and days without being found, just as they had that time they got lost. She snapped the trapdoor shut.

"It's Greta, nothing more than Greta. Greta and the horseflies."

"Horseflies my foot!" said her sister, standing up. "I'm talking about that sound of dry leaves rustling. Someone's coming this way."

The other Winterling's eyes were shining with fury, ready for battle.

"Shut your trap, scarecrow!"

They stood there listening a while longer. Tenacious, heavy flies buzzed around all over the place: in the kitchen, in the living room, on the floor and in the beds, and even inside the drawers. Greta Garbo had the advantage of having udders as stiff as carrots, always full to the brim with milk. But she had an irritable temperament, much more like a mule than a cow, and nothing infuriated her more than flies. When the flies got to her, she'd kick her hind legs and groan, sometimes biting people. But for now the cow was silent.

There was a knock at the door.

"Winterlings! Open the door, Winterlings!"

Overcome with fear (or maybe excitement), the two sisters clung to each other.

"What did they call us? Chitterlings?" whispered one of them with her nose pressed into the bosom of the other.

"Winterlings," said the other. "I think that's what they called us: Winterlings."

"Winterlings . . . " repeated the first one, pensive.

"That's right, Winterlings. And don't wipe your runny nose all over my jacket, if you please."

They started running down the staircase. Lagging behind, the first sister threw herself into the other to push her along; the second sister tried to catch her, but she couldn't. They fell down, rolled along the floor for a bit, and then got back up.

They ended up in front of the door, all over each other, bodies pressed together, without daring to open it.

They were quite different from each other, the Winterlings.

The elder one was dried-out and bony; she had a pointy face and a hooked nose. The bitterness of time passed had borne away the tenderness and sweetness of her child's heart, her faith in herself and others, leaving nothing but sheep-like inertia and a rigid routine. Closed off in her personal universe of magazines, soap operas, and melodrama, she had a single passion: an unhealthy need for security and to be left alone. For this alone she would get up, work, then go to sleep without thinking of anything else at all. And so, day after day, this is what she would call her "beautiful routine." By the time she was twenty, she looked like she was forty. By thirty-five, she looked like she was outside of time.

The other sister was remarkable for her wavy jet-black hair, her narrow figure, her fleshy lips, and above all her gaze: those green eyes with golden flecks around the iris. Her sister would raise her voice, and she'd stay quiet; she followed and kept up with her sister's timetable, not because she especially liked routine, but because it was all she had, and it assured her a tranquil life without drama and upheaval. She had always been very patient, that patience being both her best quality and her greatest weakness.

Who were they exactly? They weren't young girls. Nor were they old women. They had, however, reached the age at which they wished to live in peace. But in peace from what?

"Who's there?" they said in unison.

The cow mooed again in the stable.

4

SINCE THE WINTERLINGS HAD ARRIVED, the folks in Tierra de Chá hadn't taken an eye off them—all they did was go about spying—but no one had had the courage to come and speak with them in person.

Uncle Rosendo, the country teacher, recalled that as children they had taken a long time to learn to read. No one knew how old they had been back then. At school, they didn't play with the other children. They stuck together in the corner, with tiny spiders and butterflies hanging from their hair, in that languid and distracted way of theirs, staring at their feet as if plants or something were growing out of them.

But everyone remembered their grandfather perfectly. According to the priests, he was both devoted to the Saints and possessed by the devil. He knew of the secret herbs and plants that bloomed in subterranean gardens. According to the old folks, he was an *arresponsador*, who knew the right prayers and incantations to ward off poverty and misfortune. But according to the other arresponsadores, there was no way he could be one of them. According to some, he was dangerous; for others, he was a beast from the hereafter; and for the rest, he was no more than a humble man, equally magical and rational. What everyone *could* agree upon was that he was gifted with an acute shrewdness, such that from the first glance he could diagnose what was wrong with a sick person in front of him.

He went from house to house resetting bones, listening to the gurgling of intestines, and whispering poems to cure the evil eye. He knew how to talk to animals and how to scare off wolves. Even the mention of Don Reinaldo left floating in the air an unexpressed emotion, a deaf and mute admiration.

Because of this admiration, he came to have a large clientele, and in his last days, he dedicated himself entirely to the art of healing. Sick people from all over arrived at his house. They might be overcome by hiccups, which he cured with deathly frights, or experiencing cravings to eat stones and dirt, which was a common affliction in Tierra de Chá.

Everyone remembered the time a deaf-mute laywoman from Villafranca went into his house and came back out again reciting the Gospel and blowing kisses to the gathered crowd.

Don Reinaldo knew the secret laws that govern the relations between this world and the hereafter, and even the sciences against the evil eye, but he would speak only of simple and profound things: everyday things like nature and nothingness, fear and death. Was death a relief? Yes, death was the one true and inevitable relief of man. Death was the snow of another story.

But what Don Reinaldo knew how to do best was listen. He had an extraordinary gift for listening, and an aptitude to serve as confessor that had always provoked the jealousy of the priest, Don Manuel.

Sitting by the bed of a patient, one leg crossed over the other, he'd get out his tobacco pouch, roll a cigarette, and begin to smoke.

"Well then, friend, tell me about your kidneys," he would say.

He'd spend over an hour listening to the sick man.

The patient would tell him about all his troubles, which he would just about always blame on some external element: the winter, the rain, a wood louse, bad food, his wife, or the jealousy of a neighbor.

After listening carefully, Don Reinaldo would say, "What's happening to you is no fault of your wife, your neighbor, the winter, or even the wood louse. It's not even because of jealousy."

He was convinced that all ailments have their source in oneself. Jealousy of someone else's success, dreams, failures, a nasty thought, regret or an unsatisfied desire—these are all to do with past troubles that were never resolved. With time, these things accumulated, hardened into a cyst, and ended up as a sickness.

The cow mooed again in the stable.

"It's us," called the women at the door, again and again, "the women from the village."

But no one knew what had become of their grandfather. According to Uncle Rosendo, the country teacher, he had quite simply gone mad because of the war.

Often, as he chatted with the other men in the shadows of the tavern, Uncle Rosendo recalled Don Reinaldo's final days, when he came back simple and happy. One day, he noticed that Don Reinaldo was thinner. Two days later, he was wandering back and forth with a string of snot hanging out of his nose. He became moody, he stopped eating, he shooed away his granddaughters. He arrived at places without knowing where he was. He would stop the first person he came across and tell them, worryingly, "My feet brought me here, but I don't know where I am . . . "

This was before he disappeared for good. And before the Winterlings disappeared.

Others alleged to have seen him disappear like the wind in the cornfields, along the road that leads to Portugal.

And others still said that it was the girls themselves who had dug his grave.

Sometimes they spoke of everything from the past that related to the war in Tierra de Chá. They were times of lies and confusion. One day was white, and the next was black. One day, the villagers got up as supporters of the Left, and the next, without any scruples at all, they belonged to the Right. One day, a few of them banned the priests from accompanying the dead to the cemetery, and the next day, the very same people would declaim with fervor to the others that if it didn't rain in Tierra de Chá, or if a frost settled on the cabbages, it was because nobody prayed and God was upset. And so they'd get to praying.

One thing for sure was that the church was fuller every day, and the priest, Don Manuel, was delighted.

Even before the war broke out, Don Manuel had lost the confidence and faith of his congregation for a variety of reasons.

First, no one appreciated the way he feasted while the majority of people had nothing to put in their mouths.

Under the pretext that the church needed money for wine, holy bread, and ornaments, he went about the village pulling a cart that creaked like the devil, asking for offerings. Nobody was obligated to give him anything, but even if it were snowing outside, not a day went by without Don Manuel heading out with his cart. If there was no bread, he'd get a pail of corn, some potatoes, a wheel of cheese, a few ounces of chocolate, or a pot of local honey. He always got something.

And then there was the pungent stench he gave off. Just because he was a priest, did that mean he didn't have to wash? When you saw him coming along, you'd cross to the other side of the street.

But during the war, the church became a place of refuge for many. Some went to ask for protection from God, and others went to let themselves be seen there. One day, some of the villagers, walking by the mountain, sang something about the priests and the monks, and the beating they were going to give them. It wasn't, strictly speaking, what you might call a song, just words they made up as they went along, and that were borne off by the wind. The next day, they sang heavenly songs. They proudly wore their Saints' medals, which were covered in mold and had been found by their wives in the bottom of some drawer.

People said that if the Popular Front won, the rich folks would have to share their wealth. The poor folks liked the sound of this. But once the war started, there was no sharing of anything; instead, hunger and fear became routine.

In people's homes, anything that could be added to the bread dough that wasn't poisonous was added: straw, wood chips, toads, and stones. The village was dying of hunger; no one had anything to eat, and, even still, everybody complained about the bread and how hard it was. Folks lost a lot of teeth trying to chew on it. The Winterlings remembered that sensation, too; they'd forgotten many people's faces, but they remembered the bitter taste of the bread.

Cabbages, tomatoes, and collard greens were all scarce. Even the potato crop began to dwindle. Only the gorse bushes kept growing, fierce and solitary, unfazed by a lack of cultivation or the privations of war. They spoke of all this in the first days of the war by the hearth in their homes. While they shucked the corn, and mended or made sweaters, rumors and bits of news of a very different kind began to swirl. All of this went on, and then, after a while, they arrested Mr. Tenderlove, the dental mechanic. He was released after paying a twelve-thousand-real fine for pulling the teeth of dead people he found lying in ditches. That's what people were saying, although no one could believe it.

A few weeks into the conflict, the body of a man shot to death by a firing squad appeared by the river. By the hearth, they talked about his death with fear and anger. Some of the villagers who had voted for the Left in the elections no longer left their houses.

Several of the young men from the village were called to the front. The rest were in Brazil or Cuba, or had fled to Portugal.

When the war came, they stopped celebrating their festivals, and people began to be fearful of whom they went around with and what they said aloud.

People stopped greeting each other in the street. They met each other's gaze for a second, and then straight away looked at the ground. No one asked questions. No one understood it. No one knew if doors were open or closed, if they were heading up or heading down.

And then there was the matter of the watches. During the war, not a single watch kept the same time in Tierra de Chá. If at one end of the village a watch said it was six o'clock, at the other end it was a quarter past two.

Uncle Rosendo, the teacher, had the best time of it. He found his own personal refuge in making the children draw maps so as to be up to date with the conflict, with a well-defined border between Nationalist Spain and Republican Spain. At the head of the bodies of troops, he'd draw the arrows, the yoke, and the national flag, and sometimes he'd paste on the photo of some bigwig general he cut out of the newspaper. Next to the arrows he'd write "First Year of Triumph" or "Second Year of Triumph" or "Victory Year."

The children didn't live in fear of the war so much as in fear of Uncle Rosendo's maps.

That was when they took away the Winterlings' grandfather. They held him for a week and then brought him back home. The practice of healing and magic was banned in Tierra de Chá—it was argued they were arts of the communist persuasion—although, to tell the truth, more and more mysterious and extraordinary events took place in the village every day.

Greta the cow mooed for a third time.

"Open up, it's us, the women from the village."

One of the Winterlings opened the door.

"What do you want?" she said.

5

SO MUCH WAITING, spying from behind the curtains, deliberating over where the Winterlings could be—rumor had it they were overseas, perhaps in gloomy, rainy England. Now they wanted to know why they had come back. Above all, they were sure that the sisters would never have come back with bad intentions.

"We don't even know our own intentions," they said in unison.

And that's what it looked like. Since their arrival, each day had passed strangely in the same way for the two women. As if they'd never even left.

As if they'd always been there—with the sky, the earth, the flowers, and the moon of Tierra de Chá.

At dawn, after breakfast by the warmth of the fire (one takes coffee with milk, the other bread with wine), they link arms (one is slightly taller than the other) and leave the house, dressed in doublets, skirts, and jackets, with scarves over their heads, and clogs on their feet.

The one who breakfasts on bread and wine squints at the sky and sniffs at the air. Resting a large, bony hand on her sister's shoulder, she sighs deeply.

"Let's see what the day has in store for us," she says. Or perhaps she says, "Only God can tell what shall come to pass" or even, "Give me patience, Lord, to suffer these trials."

Which is all nonsense because nothing ever happens.

God doesn't ask patience of them nor does He put them on trial. Their strength is to be found in the push and pull of repetition.

In the village, everyone knows each other, and everyone greets each other. Each family knows everyone else's family history, the names of their parents, their grandparents, and what goods and property they own.

The village is laid out like a fishbone diagram.

It consists of one main street a bit wider than the rest running into a town square with a big stone cross. On both sides, there are alleyways clotted with dark two-story stone houses, with black stone tiles on the roofs. There's the church with its vestibule carpeted in bones, the communal oven, and the tavern. There are also carts and beasts of burden. Cows tied to a rope walk slowly over to drink from the river.

The grove of lime trees.

And behind curtains, eyes. The same eyes as always.

Everything there takes place according to the season. In summer, they thresh the grain and pick the grapes; in September, they sow and they harvest. On the evening of the first day of November, they roast chestnuts and eat them with wine. After All Saints' Day, it's the festival of the *fiadeiro* and the *esfolladas*, or the spinner and the shuckers, when all the young men and women end up dancing in the kitchen. After that comes the season to slaughter the pigs: chorizo, *zorza*. Filloa pancakes and dried apricots. All year long, they go up the mountain to collect gorse, watch over the livestock, gather kindling, and mix the manure in the square.

Always the same old faces. They are convinced that the whole world ends just around the corner from the main street, when you can no longer see the houses in Tierra de Chá.

The same faces, the same wine, the gorse, the women's stockings strangling their calves. The sweet smell of manure spread about the square.

The same signs of boredom. Everything has the same flavor as before.

The same people, and new people as well, watching the Winterlings. Watching them just to have something to do.

Among the dogs and the children, who clear a path for them, they head up the mountain, one Winterling in front, the other behind, followed by the cow and four sheep—that's all.

The women, and the animals.

The mountain.

(Their feet remember,

and they let them walk.)

They return at dusk, enveloped by the sound of cowbells. They sow some potatoes, draw water from the well, feed the chickens, grill some meat, and make soup.

They feel comfortable in this slowness. The less they talk, the better. Words entangle, confuse, and deceive; you don't need words to feel. They are comfortable, and the mere fact of being together, being alone, sharing their surroundings, a soup, an anise, makes them feel good. They do not expect more, and they do not wish for more.

Everything astonishes them: a chicken lays an egg, or a plant shoots up from among the clods of earth, and they are overcome by the certainty that God is right there.

Life seems like a miracle.

But it's not God making miracles. It's repetition.

In the evenings, while they sew on the Singer machines, they listen to a soap opera on the radio that nearly always makes them cry.

Afterward, they close the door of the house and are alone, under the covers, in the warmth of self-imposed solitude.

ONLY ON VERY WINDY NIGHTS did the routine change.

In the darkness of their bedroom, in their little iron beds, the Winterlings let themselves speak of their secret.

A voice (or is it the wind?) scratches away at the silence.

"Listen, Sala . . . "

And the other replies, "What?"

"That day, do you think . . . "

"Yes . . . "

"Do you think we did the right thing, Sala?"

"We did what we had to do, Dolores."

And then after a while: "Listen . . . "

Saladina lights the oil lamp. She stretches an arm toward the other bed and takes her sister's hand.

"What, Dolores, tell me . . . "

Her skin gives off waves of heat; the light, the beating of their hearts, and the touching of flesh soothe the women. Dolores's answer lurks in the darkness.

"Nothing."

They turn the light back off and fall asleep. At dawn, the same old fiesta. Breakfast, the cow, the orchard, the chickens, the jam,

the soap opera on the radio that makes them cry,

the *clack clack clack* of the sewing machine,

Dolores and Saladina,

remorse.

MANY THINGS IN THIS WORLD are indescribable, but the marvelous thing about the human mind is how it adapts when the worst happens. It seems to reason that beyond the worst, there can't be anything. The unimaginable has taken place, and on the other side is death, chaos, the end. But the worst thing happens, and the mind breaks through the silence. It knows how to break through. It flails around blindly, it exists in a state of shock, but it stays afloat. It rises toward the noise. It stands up and confronts. *It gets used to it.*

Remorse, a tentacular octopus.

Remorse—but for what?

Only they know.

The group of women peering in through the cobwebs in the doorway suspect nothing. Although they already know a few more things. They know what trade the sisters learned and practiced while they were away, and that they like the movies. They know that one of them married, that her husband died, and that she has no children. They know their ages: thirty and then some, maybe forty, or forty-two.

The Winterlings have offered them coffee and brandy, and have told them all of this; the women also know that they always wanted to return to their grandfather's house, the place they remembered with real nostalgia. "Having a country," they say, "means not being alone, knowing that in the trees, the rain, and the earth there is something that belongs to you, similar to blood, that even if you have gone away, it always awaits you." The women like hearing this. It forges a link.

The house and the fig tree.

The cow.

Green meadows beneath the rain.

Women from Tierra de Chá, like women all around the world, love to be told things in hushed and confidential tones, and in just the right amounts.

What they'd love to be told the most is precisely what the Winterlings no longer wish to recall. But sitting there, with their nightdresses pulled up all the way to their thighs, they feel obliged to do it: One afternoon in the summer of 1936, when they were returning from gathering gentian and chamomile from the forest, they ran into the kitchen, sure of finding their grandfather, with whom they had lived since they became orphans, sitting by the fire of the hearth. But Don Reinaldo was not there. All that was there was the big clay pot he would use to boil the herbs for his infusions, the liquid spilled across the floor. The girls understood none of it, and a few days later their grandfather returned, thin and haggard, yelling at them that they had to run away.

They put whatever they could into some rucksacks and fled through the forest. For three days, they slept there under the trees, eating wild blackberries and sucking on roots. But they didn't get very far because one of them kept thinking of the wolves, and the other of *gatipedros*, those monstrous cats with a big stone horn on their heads. They went home. Their grandfather was still there, but, after a few days, they came for him. In front of the girls, they stripped him, insulted him, and laughed at him, making him run about to avoid the stones they threw at him. When he finally collapsed, they tied his hands to a horse's tail, and dragged him off to the place where they shot him.

After that, somebody, maybe a woman from a neighboring village, took them on a bus to the port in Bilbao. She gave them some suitcases made out of cardboard. "Farewell," she said, and turned away. The girls barely knew her, but the image of that thickset woman turning her back on them and marching down the dock with great strides without turning around even a single time to look still haunts them.

Along with many other children, nearly all from the Basque country, they set off in a ship called *Havana*. They had never seen the sea; the first time they saw it was from that boat. The girls were sure the boat was taking them to Cuba, where they could pick gold coins that grew on the trees like bunches of grapes.

But after forty-eight hours of traveling, among toddlers who cried and vomited, they arrived at the port of Southampton. There were flags everywhere, and it wasn't warm at all. The day before had been the coronation of King Edward VIII of England, but they preferred to think that the flags had been put up to celebrate their arrival in Havana. All each child had were two sets of clothes and a piece of cardboard with their personal details on it. A man met them and took them to a camp. This wasn't at all how they had described it around the hearth. It rained, it was cold, and there were no talking parrots or mulattos to be seen. Nor was there gold hanging from trees. The man who had met them corrected them with a half-smile, telling them they weren't in Cuba but in Eastleigh.

They stayed at this camp for several months. They sang, danced, and were educated in the English language. They were never treated badly—or particularly well, either. When summer was over, they were separated and put to work.

One of the girls went to a house with many children. For seven pounds a month, she took care of everything around her: she washed up in the washtub using polished stones, peeled potatoes, aired out the sheets, carried trays of clothing on her head, and scrubbed the floors on her knees. She worked hard, and the lady who hired her never had reason to complain, but she was only there for a few months before they moved her, without explanation, to a different house. For one reason or another, they always ended up moving her to a different house.

The other sister worked first in a hotel making up beds and cleaning rooms, then in a restaurant, and finally in a hospital. On Sundays, the two sisters would meet up in a park, under a gray sky cleft with seagulls. They'd eat a mashed-banana sandwich, and tell each other everything that had happened that week.

This was their favorite time, because they also spoke to each other about the village. They remembered the times they would go to bathe at the river; the bitter smell of freshly cut gorse; the brilliance of the undergrowth dampened by the rain; that wolf they had found, struck by lightning; the oak groves, the fields, the voices of the Galician women; the birds in Tierra de Chá; and a madman they called the Taragoña Express because he'd run twenty-five miles a day, thinking he was a bus on that route.

When it got dark, they would go to the hotel where one of them slept, and continue talking in the shadows of the room until dawn broke. The smells of the earth and the deep mystery of the forest stayed with them. Heavy breathing, the trembling of their hands, eyes fixed anywhere but on the other's. United, they were defeated, but each found the body they sought, and the two became one. *Just let it flourish*, they thought, *then lie*.

The years went by easily, more or less in this way (after a while, a war broke out there as well), until one day when they had reached their twenties, having lived for eight or nine years in England.

Then, just when they had begun to speak the language with some fluency and had begun to take a fancy to this dull life, they were told that the war in Spain had ended some time ago, and that it was high time to return home, to get married, and find a profession.

And that's what the other women most liked hearing in the story: *to get married and find a profession.*

It comforts them and makes them feel good because, in the end, there's no need to travel so far to live the good life.

A family and a profession is exactly what they already have.

8

A PROFESSION?

A little worried, the women of Tierra de Chá ask if they, too, are *menciñeiras*, or perhaps *meigas*. Have they inherited the healing powers of their grandfather? Have they come back with a secret medicine chest and the arsenal of magical practices that, in the end, caused so many problems in the village during the war? The Winterlings reply, "Jesus, no!" and add that the women shouldn't worry because they remember nothing of that magic.

Upon returning from England, in a seamstress's workshop on Real Street, they were taught to sew on a Singer machine. Death shrouds, brides' trousseaux, embroidered neckerchiefs, and dresses for the Feast of Santiago.

To begin with, they went from house to house carrying the sewing machine on their heads, resting them on padding made from rolled-up rags. They were paid for alterations and given some dinner. Because they were good at it, they set up their own workshop. Two machines, two tables with chairs, a portrait of Generalísimo Franco, and the two women. They decided to stay for good in Coruña.

They became seamstresses.

The Winterlings hated sewing.

But things had changed a lot. It wasn't the same country they had left behind as girls. No one cared about them. Everyone had something else to worry about: a dead son, firewood for the stove, the cold, hunger. The streets throbbed with vendors, smugglers, Civil Guards, black marketeers, priests, women in pairs, and sailors. When there were queues, it meant it was the day that rationed goods like flour or oil were handed out. The rotten scent of politics had set in everywhere: in the schools, in each stitch they made while sewing, in their clothes, and in the air they breathed. The Winterlings went to courses organized by the women's section of General Franco's Falange Party, where they were told that they should behave like delicate and pleasant little ants.

And that's what they were.

Delicate little ants.

On Sundays, they went to the cinema—the only one in the whole city—although they saw the movies in fits and starts, because blackouts were frequent, and the juiciest scenes were censored.

Dolores, the prettier of the two, found a husband. He was a fellow named Tomás, a fisherman of octopus and pout whiting, who lived in Santa Eugenia de Ribeira. He had an octopus trap and a small *dorna* boat, and he set out to fish at dawn, under the stars. He had just been widowed and was looking for a woman to take care of the housework.

"Think about it carefully," her sister advised her, while she finished off a pair of pants. "Here with me, you don't want for anything. You and I make a great team"—she spat out a thread—"and what's more, once they're married, men develop bad habits. You'll see. At night, they snore . . . and ask for things."

"What sort of things?"

"You know, little things . . . You'll see. There's no reason for you to leave."

"So says the all-knowing voice of experience," answered her sister. "And what would you know about married life? I don't think there's anything strange about a man and a woman getting along . . . Anyway, you snore, too, and sometimes you ask for things. For example, just yesterday you asked me for a glass of water."

In truth, Dolores didn't quite know why she had decided on that particular fisherman of octopus and pout whiting. She had seen him on only one occasion, one day when she went to deliver a piece to a dressmaker's shop. Perhaps in marriage she hoped to find the stable life she had never had during her childhood, but the fact that it was her own sister who purported to plan out the course of her life also seemed like an insult to her intelligence.

"No, there's nothing strange about a man and a woman getting along," replied Saladina. "But you don't even know this man. And just so we're clear: the glass of water I asked you for wasn't for me, it was for my teeth."

"You're just jealous of me. Who'd ever want to marry you?"

"Oh, woman! Don't talk nonsense! If I wanted to, I could have them by the handful. It's just that I don't want to settle down . . . "

"You? Ugly and toothless?"

As soon as she'd said that she regretted it. Her sister stopped the sewing machine, *clack*, and raised her head slowly. She wore huge glasses while sewing, with frames made of mother-of-pearl and lenses that magnified her eyes. Her chin was trembling.

"What did you say?" she said.

But the other sister didn't want to repeat it. Behind those eyes protected by lenses there was only fragility, and she knew it.

They went their separate ways without exchanging another word, noses in the air. Shortly after, Dolores went to live in Ribeira with the octopus fisherman.

But one morning, only eight days after the wedding, someone knocked at the door. It was Dolores. She was much thinner, vaguely frightened, and the childhood pockmarks stood out more than ever on her scrawny cheeks.

A poor soul in a terrible state.

Her sister brought up her hand slowly, hesitantly, moving through the air and trying to reach her cheek in the gesture of a caress, or perhaps a slap.

"It's me . . . "

"Yes, yes, I see . . . " replied Saladina. With great coldness she let her in, hiding the flush of happiness that had lit up her cheeks.

They looked at each other in silence. The Winterling who had returned was hunched over and lost in her thoughts. The other one was all blown up like a toad at the sudden presence of her sister.

"My husband is at sea," she said. "I want to sew with you again."

No one asked her what had happened, and, because she wasn't given over to explanations, her eight days of marriage remained shrouded in the darkest of mysteries.

She may have marched off haughtily, but the Winterling returned with humility to the daily chores of the household. By the end of the month, she was fastened again to her comforting routine, and was once again the same old sister.

But after a while, especially at dusk, a shadow of worry descended upon her. Her sister came into the room to speak with her.

If she asked what was worrying her, Dolores would let out a long and doleful moan, like a wounded whale, from the edge of the bed.

She said that nothing worried her because she was happy as she was: a seamstress.

And if Saladina asked her if she ever regretted coming back, Dolores said she felt better as she was now: a seamstress.

And when she asked her, her voice trembling with fear (fear of the answer) if she would ever see Tomás again, Dolores would work herself into a complete panic, start bellowing, and then break down in tears.

Her weeping came from deep inside and rose up in waves, filling her mouth with the immense sound of the confusion and emptiness of her soul.

9

BUT THIS WAS ALL a part of the past, and now, at last, they were back in the village, just as they had always wanted: the distant little house, green meadows beneath the rain.

In the morning, the procession formed by the two Winterlings, the cow, and the four sheep crossed the square in silence. They passed under some apple trees in blossom, past the priest's house, and then further on past the communal oven. Then they tramped through the flower beds and into some fields that led on to the mountain.

The potholes and the stones on the road unbalanced them, but the Winterlings kept on walking straight, unshakable like the animals. "Look, there go the Winterlings and their cow with its swinging gait," people said as they walked by.

The tall one and the not-so-tall one; the pretty one and the ugly one; the one who has coffee for breakfast and the other who has bread and wine; the one with teeth and the other who lost them all biting into bread made with stones. The one who is a virgin and the other who is God knows what . . .

The one who grumbles and the other who sings.

One woman, two women. Nothing else?

(Their feet remember,

so they let them walk.)

When they reached the top of the mountain, Dolores sat on some craggy rocks. The grasslands were covered in wild strawberries, and the mountain awoke to the first trills of the birds. Along with the bottle of anise, she brought out *Superstars of Cinema*, a magazine that she bought in Coruña and that came out every month with the latest news and rumors, the movie premieres, and photos of actors and actresses from Hollywood: Humphrey Bogart, Grace Kelly, Marlene Dietrich, Clark Gable. She talked about the latest releases, the actors' weddings and divorces, and generally everything she read about in *Superstars* with the sheep and the cow. She'd ask them questions in one tone of voice and answer them herself in another.

The Winterlings had acquired their taste for cinema in England. One afternoon, in the park where they would meet up after work, a man heard them speaking in Spanish. When he found out they had arrived in England as refugees, he told them he was in charge of a production company and offered them a role in a documentary about the Spanish Civil War. It was to be called *Orphans of the Storm* and was about the settling of Galician and Basque children in Great Britain. All the lights, the cameras, the makeup . . . it was an experience they'd never forget. And they even got paid!

After this, they became interested in seeing movies. In the town where they lived, there was a single dark cinema that smelled of stale popcorn and disinfectant, and on Sundays, after eating together, they went to the evening session to shake off the boredom and the damp. Even then, they showed films in their town that would take many years to arrive in Spain: *Rebecca*, *Citizen Kane*, *Red Dust*, *Gone With The Wind* . . .

"And you've just got to see," explained Dolores to the astonished sheep, "how Scarlett O'Hara pulled the curtains right off the windows to make a dress with them . . . "

And she herself replied, "Well of course, she had no other option!"

On the mountain, the Winterlings were alone, but they felt good. "We should have been born as sheep," said one to the other. "Or as cows," her sister replied. They broke into laughter.

In the evening, they came back down the mountain, happier and chattier, tipsy from the anise. Sometimes, they sang rhymes and little songs they had learned in the camp at Eastleigh: *Baa baa black sheep, have you any wool?*

And the other sister would sing, *Yes sir, yes sir, three bags full.*

As well as their interest in movies, they had developed a unique proclivity for the lurid details of sicknesses, raped women, murders, burnt children, and all sorts of other grim fascinations. And they talked about these things while they came down the mountain, in the same slow and swinging trot as the cow.

"Do you remember," said one to the other, "when a pig bit the ear off that kid from that house up there?"

"I remember, I remember . . . I mean, here in Tierra de Chá, the pigs are bigger than the cows; they terrify us all! And do you remember when that man from Sanclás smashed into the wall and every single one of his teeth fell out?"

"You don't have any teeth either . . . "

The other one stayed silent.

"And you?" said the other, breathing in sharply. "Do you really think you're the prettiest rose in the bunch? Your bottom is quite large."

"My ass, you mean?"

"I said bottom."

"Scarecrow!"

"Don't call me that, it's so ugly!"

They both lowered their heads.

"Shut up," murmured one of them.

"Yes, shut up," murmured the other. "Right now I think we should shut up."

"Put up and shut up!" they shouted in unison, just as they arrived back at the road.

In the evening they fed the chickens, chased off snakes, sewed, and prepared a vegetable soup. They ate dinner, listened to the radio, went to sleep, and were happy. On Tuesdays, they bathed, and so, instead of sewing, they went down to the river at dusk. On Sundays, they didn't leave the house for even a moment. They cleaned it thoroughly and changed the bed linen.

Sometimes when they came down from the mountain there would be men in the square, piling up the gorse and manure to make fertilizer, and then they'd walk on with great strides (one pulled the other along by the arm) ignoring the catcalling and taunting—*baby, hot stuff*—that was directed only toward Dolores.

When they arrived at the house, on the days that this had happened, Dolores would start making dinner or fetch water from the well. But Saladina would be burning up inside. The muscles in her face would tighten, and her lips, formerly pressed together, would burst open like a flower. She'd roll her eyes and shake with laughter, a waterfall of laughter, and dash into the shed to hide, as quick as lightning.

She would re-emerge with her gaze fixed on some distant point in the countryside, serious, with a ladder over her shoulder and a set of shears in her hands. The need to repress her feelings had forged the habit of pruning.

She pruned the fig tree with such vigor that sometimes she even pulled a few tiles from the roof. The branches, the figs, *click, click,* the leaves and the tiles would fly through the air, and the chickens would run for cover.

When she had finished, the ground in the orchard would be a mash of figs and foliage. Exhausted, she would go back into the house hunched over, her face covered in snot and tears, her eyes puffy from laughing and crying at the same time. Her sister would bring her the bottle of anise and a glass, and put her feet up. Then she would go out to sweep up the branches and the mangled figs.

10

THE MOST BEAUTIFUL TIME OF DAY in Tierra de Chá was when the sun hung motionless overhead, the river was calm, and the chickens clucked after laying their eggs.

Tuesday afternoon. Off with the clogs, off with the stockings. It was bath time. Off with the skirts, and the underwear, too. Off with the doublets.

Holding hands, making energetic movements and singing loudly to ward off the cold, the Winterlings would go down to the river, hissing like cats. Once a week, if it was sunny, they lathered up from head to toe.

They scrubbed each other's waists, breasts with erect nipples, behinds like mandarin skins, and legs with abundant flesh.

One day, just as they were rinsing off their hair, pouring water over themselves with a ladle, a nauseating gust wafted over, a rancid stench like gasoline or a wet jumper.

"It's the priest," one Winterling said, sniffing the air.

Soon they heard what sounded like the creaking of an old cart.

"He's come for the offering," the other Winterling added.

They ducked down into the water at the same time, leaving only their heads above.

At first the priest didn't see them, and passed by, pulling his cart. But when he saw their clothes on a bush, he stopped and turned around.

"Daughters of God!" he exclaimed, covering his eyes with his hands. "So there you are! In the water . . . "

He walked backward, his eyes shut tightly, up to the riverbank to speak with them.

"Don't get out!" he said, sensing the movement of bodies, then hiding himself behind a bush. "What are you doing in the river?"

The Winterlings explained that they were just having a bath. Water and soap. Was he suggesting that no one in Tierra de Chá ever had a wash? In England, you didn't need to go outside to wash yourself: you could bathe indoors. Every house had a bath.

The priest listened to them, perplexed.

"And do they wash the animals in the bath as well?"

"Is he a bit simple?" whispered one of the heads in the water.

"You've come to collect the offering, haven't you?" yelled the other head. "Well, you should know you don't fool us; we don't have to pay it. We don't even go to church."

Dolores got out of the water and got dressed as quickly as she could. From the bush, Don Manuel looked without wanting to look. The first thing he noticed, when she came back fully dressed, was her hair. It was different than the hair of other women that he knew in the area. It wasn't curly, or straight, but slightly wavy. She had big eyes, almost green, with thick eyelashes, and her skin was slightly pink. A narrow waist and wide hips. And her breasts—he couldn't quite take his eyes off them.

He came out of his hiding place. He said he wasn't coming to collect an offering but rather to settle a small matter that had been bugging him lately, that had to do with the old lady who lived over on Bocelo Mountain. He bent down to adjust the things in his cart and stood there pensively. He couldn't keep it to himself a moment longer! The old woman was the devil incarnate. Making him go up every day to see her. And now she had it in her head to get back "the piece of paper." He moved the sugar so it wouldn't spill from the paper cone it came in, and stole a glance at the cabbage that the baker's wife had given him. A cabbage?

Did the Winterlings remember the old lady?

On Bocelo Mountain, near Tierra de Chá, there was a *rueiro*, a tiny hamlet, with three or four very humble houses: simple, low-to-the-ground huts in the form of boxes, with thatched roofs and beaten-earth floors, inside which there was nothing more than hearths with fires always lit, and a few cavities in the wall, dark as a wolf's mouth, with straw mattresses and patchwork quilts that served as bedding.

In one of these houses—the Winterlings remembered, how could they not?—lived an old lady with a face like a root, very small and knotty, almost a dwarf, who smelled like smoke and old blankets. She was very sick, and so every day for the last few years, Don Manuel went up on horseback to comfort her and, if things took a turn for the worse, to administer her last rites.

It could be pouring rain, the whole valley could be covered in the most insidious mist, but, early every morning, the good man rode up on his horse, zigzagging through the mountain passes, struggling with the inclines to arrive at the hut, administer holy oils, and whisper heavenly words in her ear. "Well, old girl, you're going to Our Lord."

And then, trying her hardest to show her teeth, the old lady smiled in thanks. The few teeth she had left were a filthy yellow, like horse teeth.

That day, the day he encountered the Winterlings in the river, Don Manuel had had to move his visit up. First thing in the morning, while he sipped on freshly pressed grape must in the tavern, a fieldworker came in yelling that the old woman on the mountain was barely breathing, and that the priest had to go up and give the last rites. "Oh, so she's ready to die!" he yelled back from the corner of the bar. "I was there just yesterday."

"I'm telling you, Father, this time she's dying!"

And so Don Manuel had no other choice but to finish off his must, go by his house and put the holy oils in his satchel, and head once again toward the mountain.

The rain was bucketing down. Because he thought it might be the last time he climbed the mountain, he couldn't help but feel a tiny tingle of pleasure in his heart.

When he got there, he found that, in truth, the old lady was in quite a bad way. She gave off a coarse rasping sound that was almost drowned out by the deluge outside. The priest reflected, with a certain degree of remorse, that the thoughts he had just had were hardly Christian.

"Old lady, my little old lady." Like every other day, he anointed her with oils on the eyes, the nose, and the feet, and told her that God already kept her in His glory.

Silence fell. It had stopped raining, and the sky had cleared. It was cut through with a superb rainbow. The priest saw this as a sign: God was thanking him for all his years of sacrifice.

After a while, the old lady opened her eyes. Her face was all shrunken and leathery, cracked up with tiny creases, particularly around her small dry eyes, and her nose was pointed like the beak of a bird. All she had left was one tuft of gray hair. She looked around her and, seeing the light that filtered through the cracks in the hut, sighed. "Well, looks like I'm feeling a bit better."

Hearing this, the blood rushed to the priest's face. He had already packed up his holy oils and was about to leave.

"It's time to kick the bucket, woman! Christ, that's what we're here for!" he bleated.

And then the old lady sat up, a little put off by his words.

"I can't, Father," she said.

"You can't what?"

"Die."

"Here we go. The piece of paper. You can't die because of a piece of paper you signed thirty years ago. But dying is so easy! People go and die every single day!"

The old lady asked the priest to come nearer.

"People are saying that Don Reinaldo's granddaughters are in town," she whispered to him. "That they have returned . . . "

"The Winterlings," said Don Manuel.

"Exactly," said the old lady. "Bring them to me. I have to talk to them to settle this business about the piece of paper. As soon as I have that sorted, I'll be off as quick as I can; you'll see, Father."

The old lady lay back down and pulled the covers right up to her ears.

"You're ugly, Father," she said, uncovering herself a little. "And you stink."

11

DON MANUEL FINISHED packing away the foodstuffs he had in the cart. He stood there with his fingers entwined, twiddling his thumbs.

"The old lady says she wants to see you. She found out you're back in the area, and she wants to ask something of you. She says it has something to do with your grandfather and that until it's settled, she can't go."

"Go where?" asked the head that was still in the water.

The priest stopped twiddling and exhaled through his nose.

"She keeps going on about some piece of paper she signed. I promised her you'd come with me tomorrow."

While he waited for their response, the priest set to choosing a tasty morsel from what he had in the cart. That morning he had requisitioned some filloa pancakes, bread, a pot of honey, sugar, and a cabbage (did the baker's wife think she'd get away with little vegetables now?), and he was salivating at the prospect. Climbing Bocelo Mountain had whetted his appetite.

"In any case, it's about time you came back into the fold," he added, putting a filloa pancake in his mouth. "All that business had nothing to do with you two."

He looked up, and there was the other Winterling. The exchange that then took place between the three of them was quite absurd: while the prettier Winterling made her excuses, the uglier one and the priest inspected each other like scared animals.

"The what?" said the uglier Winterling.

While he thought about the answer, Don Manuel chewed the cake with his mouth open, not taking his eyes off her.

He hadn't always been like this: it had begun with the death of his mother. The Winterlings remembered that before leaving the village, around the year 1936, Don Manuel had still lived with her. She had been a sickly and gossipy woman. Because she never left the house during the day, the mother wanted her son to tell her everything that went on in the village. And after the idiot had told her in great detail all of the most intimate secrets of confession—like a certain person's case of adultery or the lechery of another—his mother always said the same thing: "Bah, is that all you've got today? Maybe one day you'll bring me something interesting!"

But that was all part of the past; that woman was now dead, and the priest only fulfilled one role now: glutton.

"Exactly, that," repeated the priest, swallowing the filloa pancake.

"What do you mean, 'that'?"

The priest finally looked away.

"I was saying that it's time you two got together with everyone else in the village . . . "

"Are you calling us sheep?" said the Winterlings in unison. The priest took in everything with a glance: the house, the orchard, the chickens.

The fig tree twisted and sprawled over the house, its branches invading the windows without panes.

"You're very lonely out here . . . "

"We'd be even lonelier without loneliness," they replied.

"We're all sheep, or we end up becoming them. It's good to be part of the flock; it's warm and comforting," said Don Manuel, taking up the handle of the cart again. "Don't take the animals up the mountain tomorrow morning; I'll come and get you, and we'll visit the old lady."

And that's how it went. The next day, before the sun had even risen, Don Manuel was out the front of the Winterlings' house, waiting for them. When they saw him at the front door, the Winterlings wanted to flee through the back door. But there was no escape. Don Manuel had blocked the back door with his cart so that they couldn't slip away.

They had no choice but to go up Bocelo Mountain with him. While they got ready to leave, they asked him inside to sit by the hearth. But when they came down from the bedroom, Don Manuel wasn't where they had left him. They found him snooping around the stable, checking out the cow.

"The cow is fat," he said, hearing them enter.

"She certainly eats," they said.

The Winterlings sidled up slowly; then, one on each side, they gently nudged him toward the door.

"You've got a bit of a stench in here," said the priest, still scanning the stable.

"Just a regular stench," they said somewhat nervously, still nudging him. "Just a regular stable stench . . . "

But the priest wrinkled his nose to sniff at the air and did not appear to want to leave.

"The thing is, it smells foul, but not like cows or manure or even gorse. It smells like . . . "

But before he could finish his sentence the Winterlings had him outside ("*a woolly bear caterpillar*, that's what you smell of . . . "). They were ready to head up the mountain, the sooner the better, they had plenty to do—so what was he waiting for?

It was the first time they had been required to interrupt their routine, and this troubled them. Along the way, the priest wanted to make conversation. He asked them what England was like.

"Drizzly and melancholy," said one of them.

"Drab . . . " added the other, looking at the ground.

Don Manuel also wanted to know if what he had heard was true: that priests over there could get married. The Winterlings told him yes, over there priests could get married.

The priest had no further questions.

They entered the hut, lowering their heads and treading carefully. They found the old lady sleeping. Don Manuel had to shake her several times.

"I brought you the Winterlings, old lady."

The old lady smelled of smoke. She didn't even stir. She seemed despondent. The priest uncovered her roughly and began applying holy oils to her feet. She had big, cracked, dirty feet.

"Who did you say you brought?" the old lady croaked out at last.

"Here are the little girls," yelled Don Manuel. "But they're not so little anymore . . . "

Heaving herself up on her elbows, the old lady sat up to look at the Winterlings. For a good while, she eyed them from head to toe, with her tiny shining eyes.

"It's them," she said, wiping the fuzz above her lip with a sleeve. "I need the piece of paper."

Arm in arm and trembling a little, the Winterlings watched her in surprise. What piece of paper was she talking about?

And then the old lady spoke at length about the piece of paper she had signed for their grandfather, Don Reinaldo, which was now the only thing holding her back from dying. One day, when she had been sweeping the doorway to the hut, Don Reinaldo had come past on the way back from visiting a neighbor. " 'Good day, old lady, how are we?' he said. 'Terrible,' I answered. 'How so?' he asked. 'I'm so hungry I can't even think,' I told him. And then he kept on staring at me, and finally he said, 'Well, you do have a brain, old maid.' And skipping around, first behind me, then in front of me to get a better look at it, he said, 'You've got a brain like the Cathedral of Santiago.' But of course I didn't understand him. 'How would you like to leave hunger behind?' he asked suddenly. 'That wouldn't be bad,' I answered. And then he made me an offer that I happily accepted: he wanted to buy my brain to study it. He would pay me, in advance, and I just had to give it over when I died."

And so they fixed a price, and she made her mark on a piece of paper. Don Reinaldo paid her, and she was obliged to hand over her brain (in fact, someone would have to get it out for her) when she died so that he could study it. As Don Reinaldo explained to her, he was studying the furrows of, and differences between, the brains of men and women.

"But now I've changed my mind," added the old lady. "My brain is the best thing I've got; I'm not planning on heading to the next world without it. I might need it for reflecting when I'm up there. I mean, what if they have elections like we had here in '33? Fetch me that paper."

"No one is taking your brain away, woman!" interrupted Don Manuel. The whole time the woman had been talking, he had been distracted, gazing off into the countryside. "Don Reinaldo has been dead and gone for years, and what's more, it's against the law to sell organs."

"You can never be too sure," countered the old lady. "Signed papers are tricky, and a brain on the loose could get up to anything. Did you know, Father, that inside of one brain there are actually three other brains? Don Reinaldo told me that, too . . . "

She sat up a bit more. "Under here," she said, pointing with an arthritic finger beneath her mattress filled with cornhusks, "I have all my life savings. I don't weigh much. Lift me up between the three of you and then grab them. I'll return the money, and then you two can hand over the piece of paper."

The Winterlings just shrugged. They wouldn't be taking the money or looking for the piece of paper.

When they got out of the hut, the first thing the priest told them was that the story was a lie. The old dear was losing it, and, for a while now, she'd been obsessed with her brain and talking a whole lot of nonsense.

"Don't pay any attention to her," he added. "One day, she's on about the piece of paper, and then the next it's something else." He went silent for a moment, tracing circles in the dust with his foot. "So tell me the truth: Those English priests, do they have children, too?"

But that very same night, the Winterlings looked for the paper among their grandfather's things. When they had arrived in Tierra de Chá, they'd spent weeks combing through the mountain of old clothes, household knickknacks, and books about herbs and medicines that overran the attic. Everything had been thrown on the ground—brooms without sticks, broken floorboards, an umbrella, boxes full of jumbled-up papers—as if someone had been searching through there before them. Armies of bedbugs burst out of the cupboards and drawers, fleeing the light, along with notebooks, and papers with diagrams of skulls and measurements, not to mention linen and blankets reeking of kerosene, a paraffin heater, and a washbasin smashed to pieces. There was so much stuff that there would be no question of looking through all of it in one afternoon.

That night, after seeing all those insects fleeing the light, Dolores asked, "Do you remember that grasshopper we had in England, the one we called Adolf?"

"Adolf Hitler . . . Yes, how disgusting!"

Dolores remembered. How could she not?

"Maybe in the end it's not so bad being a sheep, like the priest said."

Her sister was yanking at a drawer.

"What did you say?"

"Sheep hide themselves among each other."

Her sister kept yanking at the handle of the drawer.

"Here you go with your riddles. You make me miserable, Dolores. Speak plainly."

"What I mean is," said Dolores, studying the edges of the massive drawer to help her sister, "that it's about time for us to get out of this house, to mix with the folks in the village."

Saladina stopped what she was doing and stood stiffly.

"And what about *our little secret*?" she croaked. "Might I remind you we can't just get about in the world as if nothing—"

"No one suspects a thing about *our little secret*. We are young, we have crossed borders, rivers, bridges, cities, we speak English, we've seen the sea, and we've made a movie. What will become of us, hidden away here like bedbugs and closed off from the world, with magnificent secrets inside of us, like this drawer that doesn't want to open?"

Saladina gave the drawer a yank again.

Dolores stood pensively for a moment. There was fear. Sounds that crept in from outside, from the kitchen, from the stable, a whole world of sounds: voices, noises, thuds, animals that seemed to live inside the stone walls of the house. At night they were afraid and they thought someone was scratching at the door. But it was also true that they weren't doing so badly in Tierra de Chá: The fruit from their orchard tasted better than any other fruit. The silence on the mountain in the company of the animals was invigorating. Each of them thought the other was looking prettier . . .

"If that's what you want," said Saladina, after a while.

THE OPPORTUNITY TO BECOME a sheep and blend in again presented itself on the occasion of the Festival of the Virgin. The Winterlings knew that not a single person from Tierra de Chá would be missing. And so they put on flowery dresses, stockings, fake eyelashes brought over from England, and set out on their way. They went down the main street, elbow-in-elbow, and entered the church. There, Don Manuel was preaching to his flock about fear of freedom, about slow-cooked ham with turnip greens, and about the communion of saints. Few understood him, but they all liked the words he chose. They were comforting and made them feel better.

In the first pew sat an ungainly young man, taller than he was short. They recognized him straight away: it was Little Ramón, Ramón, the maid's son who had breastfed until the age of seven. In the second pew sat Uncle Rosendo, accompanied by the unflappable Widow. A bit further back, elegant and smiling, sat Mr. Tenderlove.

The Winterlings came in, greeting the others shyly with a nod, and sat in a pew at the very back of the nave, underneath the choir stall. The parishioners drifted in in pairs, filing into the rows in front of them, staring vacantly for a short while before sitting down and letting their gaze wander to, and then settle on, the Winterlings.

They whispered.

Because it was dark in the church, the Winterlings didn't realize that "you know who" was right there, basically sitting next to them.

"It's the man who raises capons," whispered one sister to the other, elbowing her. Seeing all the villagers from Tierra de Chá up close, they thought that time had stopped again. It was true that a few small details betrayed that it was no longer 1936—such as Uncle Rosendo's gray hair, the Widow's slightly curved back, the rooster raiser's wrinkles, and Ramón, who was all grown up—but still, wasn't almost everything the same?

It wasn't the time for philosophizing. They sang the songs of their childhood until they were hoarse. Before leaving the church, Don Manuel offered a prayer to the poor and read aloud the names of those who had not taken communion this week: Mr. Tenderlove and Aunty Esteba. Then the Virgin was carried out. In Tierra de Chá, it was kept in the chapel at the priest's house, Meis's Widow was charged with the task of making a curled wig with real hair and a dress of satin and pearls for the Virgin. She got up at five in the morning to work on it and wouldn't let anyone help her.

Once the Mass and procession were over, it was time for the dancing and the feast. Twirling each other around, the women danced *airinhos* and other local dances like *muñeiras* and *jotas*. In the background, a band that had come from Pontevedra played, with a bass drum, bagpipes, tambourines, and a trumpet.

The carts had been arranged in a circle around the vestibule of the church and were selling chestnuts, loaves of bread, churros, and *rosquilla* doughnuts. There was wine as well, and the young men went back and forth to get their drinks.

The girls waited for the men to ask them to dance, and if that didn't happen, one of them would take on the man's part and link arms with the closest girl. One man gave Dolores a few slaps on the behind, and she turned around and gave him a piece of her mind.

When it began to get dark they brought out the carbide lamps, and the flickering yellow light cast nightmarish shadows.

A bit further on from the church, beneath a marquee, a woman sat at a table with her hands resting on a huge colored crystal ball. She was an old lady, with long legs, and rouge on her cheeks, and wild, stiff hair, like the bristles on a brush.

She lived tucked away on the mountain and came down only during the religious festivals to tell people's future or, in precious few cases, to warn someone whose soul she had seen that they were about to die. It was said that just by looking at someone—by the marks on their skin, their smile, or the flutter of their eyelids—she knew everything about that person, both outside and in.

Hand in hand, Meis's Widow and Uncle Rosendo approached the marquee.

"We've come to ask you how it's going to work out for us," they said shakily. The clairvoyant, whose name was Violeta da Cuqueira, glanced sideways at them, barely showing any interest.

"Violeta da Cuqueira . . . " insisted the Widow. "We've come so that you can read our future. You know, the here and the now, and the hereafter, and if . . . "

"What the Widow wants to know is if . . . " interrupted Uncle Rosendo.

"Shut it, you! She already knows what I want to know!"

The clairvoyant watched them in silence, stroking her crystal ball.

"I see two sturdy trees . . . " she said after a while.

The Widow and Rosendo responded in unison. "Oh yes?"

"Two sturdy trees, yes, maybe they're cherry trees, and new blossoms."

Meis's Widow gave a nervous giggle.

"Hold on!" Rosendo soothed her, grabbing her by the arm. "Wait and see what the old lady says . . . "

Violeta da Cuqueira clicked her tongue.

"I see children, but I can't say how many," she continued.

"Are you sure? It's just that this is my second marriage, and I'm not that young anymore."

"I'm sure," pronounced Violeta.

Meis's Widow embraced her husband and began to cry.

Uncle Rosendo clearly didn't believe this business about children.

"And do you see any mishaps or misfortune? Tell us the truth, Violeta. We're prepared for anything. Will I pass my exam to requalify as a teacher?"

Everyone in the village knew that recently, the Governor had declared that all teachers in the area still employed in country schools had to go to Coruña get certified. Uncle Rosendo had begun studying—with real books, as he told everyone—and soon the school would be closed so that the teacher could fully dedicate himself to preparing for the exam.

Violeta shifted in her seat. A trace of a sneer came across her face.

"A plague . . . of butterflies, or maybe moths, will devastate Tierra de Chá and ruin your orchard. However, this too shall pass, and the sap of the trees will double in strength."

After paying the old lady her fee, which was neither a little nor a lot, the Widow and Uncle Rosendo strode off, and nobody could tell if they were happy or sad, because they were arguing so much.

The Winterlings, who had watched the whole scene unfold, approached stealthily. They also wanted to know about their future, about their new life in the village, but they didn't dare ask.

Violeta da Cuqueira let them prowl around without saying a word. After a long while, she realized they'd never summon the courage to ask.

"You two hold a secret that crushes you like a boa constrictor, something dark . . . " she said. "I can read it in the wrinkles around your eyes."

The Winterlings gave a start.

"Oh, no!" said Saladina at once, looking around wildly, fearing that someone else might have heard. "We don't have any secrets. We're as clear as water."

"We all have secrets," said the clairvoyant. She lifted her gaze and stared at Saladina. "What's more, you . . . you are going to fall in love."

Saladina went as red as a beet.

"Saladina, in love?" said Dolores, bursting into laughter. "But she hasn't had a single sweetheart her whole life!"

"And how would you know?" interrupted her sister, elbowing her. "Let the lady speak!"

"I won't say another word about it, I'm sick of gossip," said the clairvoyant, and, raising a crooked finger, she pointed to Dolores. "I'll only say that your dream will come true."

"My dream?" asked Dolores.

"It has something to do with . . . " Violeta closed her eyes. For a few seconds, she searched the depths of her mind. "It has something to do with show business. Are you a dancer?"

Now it was Saladina's turn to burst out laughing.

Dolores told her no, she wasn't a dancer.

"Are you an actress?"

Dolores felt her blood run cold.

"Yes, I am . . . well, no . . . but I love movies. We both love them, that's for sure!"

"Well, that must be it. Your dream has something to do with the movies."

Violeta da Cuqueira wouldn't say a word more. She also refused to charge them, despite the fact that the sisters already had their purses out, delighted by what they had heard. The old lady got up, wrapped herself in her cape, and stalked off.

The Winterlings watched her disappear through the lemonade stands and the strings of doughnuts, melding into the throngs of people and hidden by the shadows.

With her crooked fingers up in the air, she looked just like a witch.

"ROLL UP FOLKS, roll up and see the donkey who can read a newspaper! A literary superstar, here in person!" A bit further down from the vestibule of the church, there was a tent where some carnies—the very same ones who years ago had brought the Bearded Lady—had installed a donkey that knew how to read. Every single person from Tierra de Chá filed past, each paying three pesos to see such a wonder.

The Winterlings looked on, astonished. They recalled that one day, in England, they had seen a bear strolling through the streets with its keeper, with a chain leading to a ring through its nose. But this was a thousand times more fascinating, because this animal had wisdom. They had their money out, ready to pay—afterward they would be able to say, when they went to visit Coruña, that in Tierra de Chá they had donkeys that could read—when it occurred to them to ask the people coming out the back door of the tent if the claims about the donkey were true. By chance, the next one out of the tent was Little Ramón, Esperanza's son.

The same big head with the tiny ears like cherries. As they understood it, as soon as he could, he got out of the village. Now he was a sailor, and he spent great stretches of time away. He only came to Tierra de Chá for the religious festivals.

Ramón stood there admiring Dolores, then he told her that he remembered her and that, not long ago, he had seen her in Ribeira.

"In Ribeira?" she asked, blushing. "I was only in Ribeira for a short while. I always lived with my sister in Coruña. We had a workshop on Real Street. No, we haven't seen each other since we were kids. Do you remember how we used to play together?"

Ramón wore a moustache and had big, uneasy eyes.

"You married Tomás, and you went to live in Ribeira," he said without answering the question. "I was at your wedding. I've never seen such a look of fear in my life."

The Winterlings cast each other sidelong glances.

"Jesus!" said Saladina quickly. "What nonsense! You must be confusing her with someone else. My sister was only passing through Ribeira, like she just told you. We prefer Coruña . . . "

"It's been quite a while since I've seen Tomás," continued Ramón thoughtfully. "When I head back, I'll have to go and visit him. What happened? Did you run off? Tomás has a reputation for being difficult."

They were interrupted by the voice of the carny: "Ladies and gentlemen, come in and take a look, last call for tickets to see and hear and the donkey who reads!" They all stood silently.

"Well then," said Dolores. "I do believe we are going to see this donkey."

"Yes," agreed Saladina. "We're going to take a look at this wonder of nature."

"But of course," said Ramón, without taking his eyes off Dolores for a moment. "You were asking me if it's true that the donkey reads. He does. He reads splendidly. And what's more, he's also a doctor, or a chemist."

Without thinking twice, the Winterlings paid their three pesos and entered the tent. They stood leaning against the wall for a while, taking stock of the conversation they had just had.

The donkey was on the other side of the tent, very calm, with spectacles and a straw hat, from which a few plastic flowers dangled.

In front of him was an open newspaper. They waited for a while, and nothing happened. But just as they were considering going out again and asking for their money back, they heard the donkey clear his throat (he crowed, more like a rooster than a donkey) and recite, in a clear voice, an advertisement from the newspaper: *Pautauberge Solution. The most effective remedy against chest infections, recent and persistent coughs, and chronic bronchitis.*

It was the most solemn and velvety voice they had ever heard. When he said the line about the "chronic bronchitis" he didn't sound like a doctor, he sounded like a bishop. Saladina's heart leapt. When the donkey had finished reading, she approached him. She thrust herself forward courageously—normally, she would never speak to someone she hadn't met before, much less a donkey.

"Hello, little donkey. I'm Sala, Saladina, the seamstress, and it's a pleasure to meet you. I greatly enjoyed your reading, and I would be delighted to listen to you more often," she whispered.

The donkey shifted in his seat. He raised his head and looked at the bewildered Saladina through his spectacles. His eyes were glassy and bulging like those of a fish.

"Even dressed as a donkey I wouldn't spend time with you, you hag!" pronounced the same velvety voice that had read the newspaper.

Saladina stood there frozen and smiling, like a stuffed animal, not knowing what to do. When she got out of the tent, she had to grab onto her sister's arm to avoid falling over. She said she wanted to go home.

Just then an excited young man interrupted them. He was thinking about going into the tent, and wanted to know if it was true that the donkey could read. Summoning the last of her strength, Saladina took two steps forward to answer.

"He reads splendidly. Even the most complicated sentences. And he's also a priest or a chemist."

Although the donkey's words weighed on Saladina as the worst of all possible humiliations, her sister, who hadn't quite heard everything that had been said, managed to convince her not to leave. For the rest of the festival, the Winterlings went from group to group introducing themselves.

When the others heard them exchanging words in a language they didn't understand, they asked them what language it was that they were speaking. The Winterlings said it was English, but the villagers of Tierra de Chá couldn't believe it. An Englishman spoke English, a Frenchman spoke French, and someone from Portugal spoke Portuguese. They couldn't understand how the Winterlings, who weren't English at all, could speak that language.

They also asked if it was true that over there, in England, priests could get married. The Winterlings told them that they could, because they were Protestant.

Don Manuel, the priest, who was also very interested in that particular conversation, came over.

"And is it true that all Protestants have tails?"

The Winterlings told him that they did. England was full of beautiful cathedrals and Protestants with tails.

"And what about teachers? Do they have country teachers in that land, or have they not gotten certified yet?" chimed in Uncle Rosendo.

The Winterlings told him that they had no idea, but that they supposed that all the teachers had studied extensively and had many degrees, because they didn't fool around in England. When he heard this, Rosendo felt his legs turn to jelly with fear.

While a man approached Dolores to ask if he might buy her some churros, or invite her to dance, and she told him no, no thank you, she wasn't hungry or thirsty or in the mood for dancing, she saw that her sister had slipped away from the crowd and was stumbling through the darkness of the vestibule until she could stop and lean against the wall of the church. A few minutes later, the dental mechanic, Mr. Tenderlove, came up to her. He was the only man who had shown an interest in her all night long. When she spoke to him, Saladina looked at the ground. What could they be talking about?

On the road home, Saladina again felt the sharp sting of humiliation. A group of young men came up to flirt with Dolores, passing Saladina by as if she didn't exist. And although Dolores couldn't help but feel flattered, she kept on walking as if she hadn't heard a thing, so that her sister, who hadn't been asked to dance all night, wouldn't feel offended. But as they walked past the very last of the houses, she noticed that the blood had risen to Saladina's face, and by the time they reached the apple trees, she had crumpled into tears.

"Why are you crying, woman?" asked Dolores. "If those men didn't notice you, it's because you're not useful to them. It's true! I should be the one crying. Listen, I'm still worried. Do you think Little Ramón knows anything about our little secret?"

"It's because of my teeth," spluttered Saladina, ignoring the question. The tears were running down her cheeks and pooling on her shoulders. "Everything that goes wrong for me is because of my teeth. People notice that they're fake, and it's disgusting."

"They're just teeth—God!"

"They're disgusting, I'm telling you! I'm a toad!"

"You're a thousand times better than a toad, and that's why you have to wait for your chance. You heard Violeta da Cuqueira; you'll fall in love soon."

This last comment, the only intention of which was to lift her spirits, was a true insult to her sadness; Saladina's eyes rolled back, and she began to sway.

With huge strides hurried by embarrassment, with sweaty palms and a stiff body, she managed to get to the house. Then she went straight to the shed. She came out with the ladder and the shears, climbed up, and, by the light of the moon, began to prune the fig tree.

Click, click.

She didn't come down off the ladder until there were no more branches left to prune.

"Here we go," her sister consoled her, taking her arm and leading her inside like a little girl. "It's bedtime now."

14

SALADINA WAS SO EXHAUSTED that she gave in and let Dolores help. Her sister took off her dress and put on her nightdress. She let down her hair, removed her dentures and placed them in a glass of water, then put her to bed and pulled up the covers lovingly, telling her the story of Taragoña Express, who ran all over the countryside wearing nothing but a loincloth.

Just when it seemed that she was going to fall asleep, she poked her head with its wild hair out of the sheets. She stretched out her arm, grabbed the dentures, and put them in, *plop*.

"Well? Did you like being a sheep?" she asked through her sniffles.

Dolores shrugged. She was used to her sister's ironic turns and wasn't surprised by the question.

Saladina jumped out of bed and got down on all fours.

"*Baa, baa, black sheep, have you any wool?* They're nothing more than sheep!"

"You're all worked up, Sala, calm down . . . "

"And did you notice, Dolores, that no one wants to talk about our grandfather?"

Dolores didn't answer.

"As soon as you bring it up, they go silent and start fidgeting. And then there's this business about the old lady's piece of paper. Do you think it's true that our grandfather bought her brain?"

Dolores didn't know what to say. She opened her mouth and

kept it that way, as if she'd been interrupted. Saladina got up and sat down on the bed.

"And this nickname they've given us, the *Winterlings*, how about that . . ."

"They give nicknames to those who keep secrets in all villages," reasoned her sister. "It makes sense."

"Yes, it makes sense."

"Because of *our little secret* . . ."

They heard a noise coming from the stable. Dolores opened the trapdoor and had a look. She spent a while with her head hanging down through the hole, looking and listening carefully. "It's just Greta," she said. "The horseflies are eating her alive."

They sat in silence. The crickets began chirping. Saladina's face was shiny with sweat, and she was very agitated.

"I was talking with Mr. Tenderlove," she said suddenly.

"I saw you."

Saladina's throat gurgled like a blocked pipe.

"You saw me?"

"I saw you."

"I see. Well, listen, Dolores . . . what if I got some new teeth?"

Dolores gave her a prolonged and penetrating look. Then she set about folding the sheet back under the mattress. Sitting next to her sister, she felt her body's welcoming and friendly warmth. It wasn't love that she felt for her. Affection, tenderness perhaps. But really, what kind of nonsense was she on about. How could she not love her? Her bad moods were exasperating, her grunting and her shrill voice as well, but it was a gift to have someone to laugh and talk with every day. Saladina needed her, almost like a mother, and Dolores hung on to that need. She *needed* that need. That was it, plain and simple.

She would never again confuse her feelings. Once had been enough.

With a quiver of fear, she remembered that night, two or three days after they had arrived in Tierra de Chá. They had just gone to bed; it was that time of night when the colors in the sky settle and the stars are pulsing. Through an animal or even biblical instinct, they had realized that they needed to feel each other. They tore off their nightdresses, knocked over the nightstand, and pulled the little iron beds together, coming together in a warm embrace.

They were intimate with each other only once.

Beneath the crucifix and the smiling portrait of Clark Gable, the mattresses filled with cornhusks creaked away through the night.

The next day, they were embarrassed. They apologized to each other: "Forgive me." "No, you forgive me." "Forgive us both, Clark."

They didn't speak to each other again until nightfall the next day.

It never happened again.

Now Saladina was waiting for an answer. Aside from the tense expression she had when she was alone—when she sewed or when she threw the feed to the chickens and she thought no one was watching—she had one other expression, which was of patient expectation, in which she pressed her lips together with a horrible noise, her upper dentures fixed between her tongue and the roof of her mouth. This was the expression she wore at that moment.

"New teeth, you say?"

It wasn't love she felt; it was fear. Because sometimes fear shows itself in unpredictable ways: it can be monstrous affection. That's what had happened that night. Fear breeds confusion. When the worst things occur, fear bewilders you. Dolores needed her sister's obsessions, her ascetic discipline, her way of being in the world, somewhere between madness and the void. There was a mixture of chaos and order in Saladina that fascinated her.

Greta the cow let out a long moo from the stable.

With so much going on, no one had remembered to milk her.

15

AT THE SAME TIME, Mr. Tenderlove entered his office. His house
was behind the village, tucked away in the trees of the forest. To
get there you had to walk down a road lined with chestnut trees
that ended up at a stone building eaten away by moss and silence.
Upstairs he had his office, a spacious and airy room that he used as
a kind of laboratory.

As soon as he switched on the light, a sense of pleasure took
hold of him: the gratifying tingle of knowing that this was his space,
his little nest, his home. Just like every other night, he prepared
to take stock and clean his equipment. On top of that, he wanted
to check if he had all the pieces he had chosen in his mind for the
Winterling.

Saladina the Winterling.

Next to the revolving chair where the patients sat there was a long
table with drawers of different sizes. From one of them he pulled
out a brush, some scissors, a file, and a hammer. From another,
slightly larger drawer he slowly pulled out the spatulas, the calipers,
and the prostheses. This was always the first thing he did; he loved
having the table overflowing with things. His objects mitigated the
void, making him feel better, because deep down he knew that he'd
never learn to live alone. He slowly placed the instruments on the
tabletop and counted them. Then he stood up on his tiptoes to look
at himself in the mirror that hung from the wall. He shook his head
and a lock of hair came loose. He tried a half-smile, and, making a

face he'd never tried before, not even in front of the mirror, he told himself that yes, nearly all of them were there.

As a young man, Tenderlove had been active in the Popular Front and had dreamed of redistributing wealth and changing the world. But when the war started, after he was arrested and tortured, he understood that this was an impossible ideal and that there was no point getting caught up in a battle that he was bound to lose anyway. He swore he would never again meet with anyone who had anything to do with politics, and fell back into his work.

His father had been a good mechanic and had taught his son everything there was to know about the craft. But ever since he was a child, Tenderlove had shown a dark passion for dentures. He knew each and every mouth in Tierra de Chá: dark pits where teeth sharp like a crocodile's rotted away; hills separated by valleys and topped with golden crowns; unfathomable and decaying grottos; fixed and hanging bridges; caves like a great abyss, with stones and pebbles that gave off a putrid stench. Soon enough, he realized that his future lay in those toothless mouths.

And so one day, when he was helping his father fix a motor, he thought of combining his knowledge of mechanics with his passion for the mouths of others.

Soon after the war broke out and he was arrested, he was transported in a covered wagon with a dying comrade, who asked him to take a love letter to his wife as a final favor. In return, the man said, he could keep his gold tooth when he died, seeing as he had nothing else to offer. Tenderlove didn't think he'd be able to pull anyone's teeth, much less those of a comrade from the Popular Front, but when the poor kid died, he got out some pliers and, one by one, pulled out all of his teeth, which he then kept in his pocket.

When he returned to Tierra de Chá and delivered the letter, he began his new life. While his former comrades joined the underground resistance, stealing through the mountains of Galicia with their rifles and daggers, he set about putting together the set of teeth he had been keeping in a glass of milk. He never told anyone where he got the teeth. In the meantime, he observed people's mouths and learned all he could about chewing and swallowing.

At the Festival of the Virgin, Tenderlove and Saladina had spoken at length. As soon as he saw her he noticed that she used false teeth, and while he didn't make any direct comments, to avoid hurting her pride, he did tell her that in his house he had some teeth that were as white as Japanese pearls—teeth he'd made himself, he clarified—so that he could make a set of false teeth on his own at any time.

The idea of getting new dentures seemed frivolous to Saladina at first. Then, after she'd thought about it for a while, she realized that plenty of other people in Tierra de Chá had done it. Mr. Tenderlove's reputation for skill was such that it was almost fashionable in the village and the surrounding area to have your real teeth pulled and dentures put in.

"New teeth like Japanese pearls," she explained to her sister, her eyes wide and shining. "New teeth, Dolores. Don't you think it's a good idea? What do you say?"

Dolores stared at her. It had been quite some time since she'd seen her sister so excited. Little by little, life had taken her dreams away from her, and since they had returned from England, she barely enjoyed anything. Her eyes lit up with irony.

"Get them," said Dolores.

"You really think so?"

Dolores had always understood that her sister's dissatisfaction stemmed from this absence, from the shame of having lost her teeth when she was little more than a child.

"Go for it."

16

WHEN SALADINA WALKED into Tenderlove's office the next day, she found the dental mechanic with a magnifying glass in his left hand and a file in his right. The task of filing down teeth so that they fit snugly took the concentration and patience of a Benedictine monk, and for this reason he didn't hear her.

He didn't sense her presence either until she touched his arm.

Tenderlove dropped one of the calipers onto the floor.

"Winterling!" he said. "I wasn't expecting you so soon."

Saladina stood there mutely.

"I knew you'd come along in the end, everyone eventually does, but—so soon!"

She nodded timidly. By the light of day, Tenderlove was much more attractive than when she had seen him at the festival. He wasn't too tall, he was well dressed and tan, and he had a muscly build and curly hair. He used brilliantine in his hair and parted it to one side, plastering it to his skull. He smelled faintly of jasmine, or was it roses? His shirt was partly unbuttoned, showing his chest. There was something deeply brooding and mysterious about him that made Saladina step back a little and wait for him to give instructions of some sort.

"Don't worry, young lady. I already told you that nearly everyone in the village has my teeth. That bread they made with stones during the war caused a lot of grief. Take a seat."

He sat her down in the swivel chair.

"I was already picking out the teeth for you. Open your mouth."

Saladina opened her mouth.

"Take those dentures out."

Saladina closed her mouth.

"I can't," she said. "I'm ashamed to be seen without them. I look like a toad."

Taking advantage of her open mouth, Tenderlove stuck in the pliers as she spoke, yanking the dentures right out. He held them up to his eyes and inspected them carefully. She instinctively clutched her sore cheek.

"Some people make them so poorly. They think that just putting them in white is the whole job," he said. "They have no respect at all for the bone. That's what it all comes down to: the bone. The bone is the beginning of all things, it is love, it is the essence of life. You must scrape and scrape until you get to the bone . . . "

Saladina listened, captivated.

"Where did you buy them? They say you two were in England . . . Never mind. I'll fix your mouth up like God intended. You'll have to come for thirty-two days, that's the number of pieces we have to install, sixteen in each jawbone. Eight incisors to cut through food, four canines, which are used for tearing food, eight premolars for chewing, and twelve molars for grinding . . . "

The Winterling nodded her head.

"It's laborious because I have to put them in tooth by tooth, but it's worth the trouble. You know, there have been people who already had a set of dentures in good condition and decided to change theirs for mine."

"I heard that," said the Winterling. "To be honest, it's strange that a man like you, who knows how to make these marvels, still has the same set of teeth you were born with . . . "

"Well, there's a lot we could say about that. But back to the point: it's clear you need new teeth. Tomorrow you can—"

"My sister was asking"—she interrupted again—"what the teeth are made of?"

Mr. Tenderlove had an answer ready for her; in fact, it was the same one he had given to everyone he had made dentures for previously.

"A friend of mine brings me the material; it's titanium. It never rusts. It never breaks. It's extracted from sand at the beach. Here in Galicia, there is plenty of titanium."

"Ah . . ."

The dental mechanic wound up her visit and went on with his task of filing down the teeth. Just as Saladina went out the door, he called to her: "I remember when you were a little girl. You were very . . . shy. You were very pretty." He raised a hand and brushed a brilliantined lock from his forehead. "And you still are. I always believed that behind your shyness there was something, something that made you special and different from the other girls."

Saladina gave a start. There was nothing in her sweaty face or bony disposition that indicated that his comment had affected her, but she was boiling inside. She felt deliciously wild. Her, Saladina the Boring—what was happening to her? For the first time in her life, someone had discovered the truth, *her truth*.

But then, straight away, she thought that perhaps the dental mechanic had confused her with her sister . . .

She couldn't open her mouth. The words were there, but her mouth wouldn't open.

"What's more," continued the dental mechanic, "I believe that your grandfather was an exceptional person, an intelligent man who just wanted to learn. On many afternoons, he would bring me figs and stay chatting . . . How good those figs tasted! Do you still have the fig tree?" Tenderlove shook his head gently. "No, he didn't deserve what happened to him . . . "

Saladina didn't understand.

"My grandfather?" she spluttered. "What happened?"

"He was a good man . . . "

Tenderlove leaned over the table and got down to filing a little tooth.

Then Saladina explained very excitedly everything that the old lady on the mountain had told them.

"She says that my grandfather kept staring at her and finally said, 'Old lady, you've got a brain like the Cathedral of Santiago.' And then afterward, he made an offer that she gladly accepted: to buy her brain. He would buy it for his research, and she just had to give it up when she died. The old lady accepted. They set a price and the old lady made her mark on a piece of paper. My grandfather paid her, and she committed to hand over her brain for his investigations when she died. What do you make of that?"

Mr. Tenderlove kept filing down the tooth.

"Did you already know that story?" asked Saladina.

"It's a story that lives on in this village," answered the dental mechanic after a while. "Everyone has heard it told—minding the cows in the meadow, baking the bread in the oven, in the tavern, at the entrance to the cemetery or by the stone cross—and everyone tells it, too. They say the contracts are in a wooden box. The whole story could've been forgotten by now or left floating in someone's house if it weren't for that old lady who just won't die. Don't pay attention to her!"

The dental mechanic suddenly went silent.

"I have to get back to work now," he said. "Tomorrow morning at ten. I'll be waiting to put in your first tooth."

Saladina nodded, confused.

"Winterling, I forgot to tell you . . . For your next visit . . . "

Saladina smoothed her skirt and ran her hands through her hair. "Yes?"

For a few seconds, all that could be heard was the sound of the file. While she awaited his response, the Winterling's gaze dropped slowly to the floor. Then she noticed that from the cuff of the dental mechanic's pants, the tip of a shoe was pointing out. A red woman's shoe.

"Don't eat any garlic or onions."

17

DOLORES WAS RESTING her temple against the cow's flank and staring off into the distant countryside when she saw her sister arrive, looming large then small as she advanced through the cornfields.

Saladina entered the house like a flash of lightning, showing all the signs of great excitement. Dolores finished milking and followed her with the pail.

"It's true!" said Saladina.

Dolores left the milk in the kitchen and hurried to attend to her sister. Saladina was radiant, her cheeks burning from the journey. She took her bag, removed her shawl, helped her put on her robe, and knelt down to put on her slippers. She accompanied her into the kitchen.

"What's true, woman?"

"All that business about our grandfather. He bought brains, it's a story everyone knows. Not just that old lady from Bocelo; the whole village sold him their brains."

Dolores started up the Singer sewing machine. While she sewed, she listened carefully, both perplexed and doubtful.

"The contracts are in a wooden box. The dentist told me." Saladina began to look about wildly from side to side, her hands in the air. "Let's look for them!"

Dolores said that they'd already searched and that the story about the brains was outrageous, nonsense from a crazy old lady. The priest himself had said so.

"But the priest sold his brain, too!" Her sister was screeching and stamping her feet. "It was the most expensive one!"

Saladina was already searching. She looked in the kitchen, in the living room, and in the stable. Then she went up to the attic and started pulling at the locked drawer that they still hadn't managed to open. From inside the drawer came a knocking sound: *plonk, plonk*.

Dolores the Winterling kept on sewing downstairs. *Clack, clack. Plonk, plonk.*

Finally, Dolores got up and offered to help Saladina.

They turned the house upside down without finding a single thing.

In the evening, sitting in front of the Singer, they began to doubt Tenderlove's words. It wasn't unusual for people in small villages to make things up, or get confused . . .

The next day, Saladina returned to the dental mechanic's office to have the first tooth inserted. That day she had risen early, even before Greta the cow began to moo in the stable. Sitting at the kitchen table with pencil and paper, the tip of her tongue poking out, she set out to make a list of all the names of teeth she could remember Mr. Tenderlove mentioning. On one side, in the left column, was the name of the tooth, and in the right-hand column, its function: incisor-*cut*, canine-*tear*, premolar-*grind*.

Next, she climbed the ladder to gather some figs. The sweetest ones were very high up, and she had to stretch from the top rung to reach them. Dolores watched her from below, while she scattered the feed for the chickens. Saladina stumbled and was left hanging from a branch. Dolores let the plate with the chicken feed fall to the ground and eventually climbed up the ladder and rescued her sister.

"Look, all the feed is spilled on the ground," she said once she had gotten back down again. "One of these days you'll be the end of me. And just so you can take some figs to this dentist-quack of yours . . . "

But Saladina's visits to Mr. Tenderlove's office weren't the only new thing. As the days went by, the Winterlings began to abandon their stifling routine and take on new habits. They began by cheerfully greeting anyone who stopped them on their way to the mountain.

"So, what are you up to? Heading to the mountain?"

"We're heading up there, yes," they would always reply, "and why wouldn't we be?"

They soon learned as well that each village has its own foibles, its moods and rules for belonging, and that company has its price: they had to bend to the customs of the community. Visiting certain places meant *always* visiting those certain places, or they'd remain alone.

To be a part of the community in Tierra de Chá, you had to go every evening to the tavern, a dive smelling of must and loneliness with a low roof, attended by a redhead and his wife, who were always leaning on the worm-eaten bar. There was no point passing by every once in a while. At six o'clock every evening, either you were in the tavern or you weren't. Among the sticky fly-strips that hung from the walls, folks got together to play card games like *la brisca* or *tute*, have a few drinks, watch television, and tell each other stories.

On the counter there was an oil lamp, and hanging from the wall there was a calendar with a faded photograph of the Pope. The redhead, leaning forward slightly, listened carefully to the conversations around him. His wife, her eyes on the television, rinsed out the empty soft-drink bottles in a bucket, making faces.

There were only two television sets in the whole village: one belonged to the priest (although he denied it and kept it hidden), and the other one was in the tavern. It was an old piece of junk that gave off a blurry picture in black-and-white and worked well enough to bring in the customers.

Uncle Rosendo used to sit at a nearby table, on a cask or old crate. He'd arrive at around four o'clock, when his classes finished, and begin ordering drinks. Little by little, his cheeks lit up, his nose turned red, and his eyes went shiny. He began to recite poetry and talk nonsense. At seven o'clock on the dot, the cask he'd been sitting on would roll backward with a crash, and he'd be laid out on the ground like a toad.

That was when the innkeeper would send word to Meis's Widow.

Every afternoon went the same way.

Boom, and the innkeeper would send word to the Widow, who, in fact, was no longer a widow.

His wife would come in their wagon, loaded with freshly cut grass, pulled along by the cow.

"I'm telling you I saw her myself last night, she was flying!" sputtered Uncle Rosendo, referring to his wife, who was coming through the door. "Flying above our marriage bed!"

"You ought to stop drinking!" yelled Tristán from another table. "Christ, if I had as much free time as you . . . If my birds didn't keep me to such a tight schedule . . . The amount of things I could get done! Don't you realize that the booze is making you see things?"

"That's not true, we only see what we already know," replied Uncle Rosendo solemnly.

Tristán, the other man, would never be able to understand such a deep philosophical thought.

"You shouldn't be drinking; you've got your exam soon. Have you studied all the lessons?"

For a moment, Rosendo was transfixed. He thought of his wife's face, which looked like a bedbug. He realized that the worst thing in the world that could happen to him would be to fail the exam, because he'd never have the courage to return to Tierra de Chá. He'd have to sleep in the flophouse, in a room that smelled like used towels.

But after a moment, he came out of his trance.

"There are those who do things, and there are those who tell others what they should do. You, Tristán, belong to the second group. I'm telling you I saw the Widow flying, just like a witch."

"How about a bit of respect for your wife!" came a call from across the tavern.

But Uncle Rosendo had no respect at all for his wife. He was convinced that the Widow was pleased that he got drunk every afternoon, because deep down, he knew that what pleased the Widow most was exactly what she said displeased her.

He had all kinds of theories for explaining life, and for exploring the labyrinth of his wife's mind; it was himself that he failed to understand.

In the first place, he couldn't understand why he had married a woman like her—so different from him—who did nothing but talk about her deceased husband. Meis's Widow: if people still called her that, it was because, in truth, that's how she behaved. Sometimes, when she wasn't paying attention, he followed her around the house. When she went into the living room, she would speak to the portrait of her dead husband and blow him kisses.

She was as ugly as Satan. Her skin was the color of ash, and her hair stuck to her face. The worst thing was that she wasn't affectionate at all. Not even when she came to pick him up in the wagon would she show a hint of tenderness. Every morning,

Uncle Rosendo woke up and asked himself what he was doing with this woman who hadn't even stopped mourning her previous husband. He'd consider leaving her, and yet, when night fell, he still hadn't done it. He would get drunk, and she would come and get him in the wagon. Life—not people or things—imposed its way on the world, and no matter how he tried, he couldn't change a thing.

As a young man, Uncle Rosendo had known other women, but he always knew he would never marry. He got to know the Widow around the hearth at the Winterlings' house, when Don Reinaldo was still alive. Recently widowed then, she would purse her lips as if blowing kisses into the air, and he would respond by blushing deeply and taking off his cap. After the war, everything happened very quickly. In the afternoons, the Widow would wait for him by the fountain in the square. He was the country teacher, and while they listened to the sound of water falling he would speak to her of poetry, of geography, and even of philosophy.

"Please stop," she would interrupt, placing her palm over his mouth. "I've never been one of those women of letters. I don't even like books."

"Well, you should hear one of Rosalía de Castro's poems, 'Adiós, adiós, prenda do meu corazón,' " he would reply, winking. "By the way—what's your name?"

"The Widow. Meis's Widow."

"I know that's what they call you, but that's not a name. What's your real name?"

"Well, I haven't got another one. You're not an uncle either, but everyone calls you that."

"Give me a kiss."

"No way! My husband might see us."

Back then, Uncle Rosendo thought she was losing her marbles. He didn't understand why he was attracted to a woman like her, who was only interested in her dead husband.

"Your husband is dead."

She frowned.

"So what?"

Uncle Rosendo was made of other stuff; this was obvious to everyone. He was twenty years old the first time he heard a poem. As a matter of fact, it was by the Winterlings' grandfather's hearth that he had heard it. He couldn't remember who had read it; perhaps it was one of Don Reinaldo's friends—he was visited by mayors, lawyers, poets, and unionists back then—or perhaps it was Don Reinaldo himself.

The poem was about the passage of time, about love and solitude, or something like that. Things that are simple but profound—you never know quite what a poet speaks about, because the poet always speaks of himself. But while he listened to those words (cold, birds chased by the light, lime, and liver) he began to feel a strange tingling all over his body. When the reading was over, he remained by the fire, unable to take his eyes off the spot where the man had read, his cheeks flushed. He was startled.

Until then, Uncle Rosendo had never thought that things like the passage of time, solitude, lime, and livers could move one profoundly. Until that man had spoken of it in such beautiful words, he hadn't known that love could be a source of disquiet and that life was an extraordinary thing.

And life *was* an extraordinary thing. He began to read poetry and teach it to the children. Without realizing, he was teaching not only poetry but all kinds of universal knowledge—from the moment when Eve felt the urge to eat fruit in the Garden of Eden and stretched her arm out for an apple, to the time of Napoleon and his tumultuous Carlist wars. There were bits and pieces of arithmetic, the names of the continents, and the names of some African animals, like the lion and the giraffe. Some parents paid him with packages of flour or corn, while others wondered about the point of literacy, given that there was absolutely nothing in the village to read.

He set up the school in the hayloft of his own house. On the outside he put up a sign that said "Tierra de Chá Children's School," and beneath that "Uncle Rosendo, Country Teacher." He brought in snakes and bats to show the children. "There's something in my coat pocket for you," he would tell them. And the children, who came from all over, walking on the paths through the forest, would put their hands inside. The only reason he taught was because he himself wanted to keep learning.

He also discovered that poetry was favored by the type of woman he had always fancied, but that had never fancied him.

One day shortly after this, the Widow came into the barn. She said that she didn't like poetry, but that she was impressed by the school. Rosendo began trembling. Without knowing why, he threw his cap to the ground, yelled out "Jeepers!" and pushed the Widow to the wall, trying to kiss her.

"Not until we're married," she said without much surprise, disengaging herself.

"What difference does that make?" he asked, perplexed.

"My husband might see us."

That was when Uncle Rosendo declared he'd never speak to that crazy woman again.

They got married in the village church—the same one in which she had married the first time—on the same day of the same month, because the Widow said that they wouldn't offend her husband that way.

At the reception, when it came time for dessert and cigars, she disappeared. After looking for her everywhere, they found her washing herself in the reservoir. Her explanation was that she was telling her dead husband how it all had gone.

Also to avoid causing offense, she refused to get married in white, and she didn't even take off her black mourning shawl on her wedding night. On this occasion, Rosendo held his tongue.

The Widow had told him that the mourning period for a grandparent was a year, for a sibling it was two, for a parent it was three, and for a child or a spouse, a lifetime. And so, out of respect, he didn't say anything. He knew a fair amount about geography, algebra, and poetry, but he didn't know enough about that gray illness of the mind called mourning to venture an opinion.

Uncle Rosendo had envisaged that marriage would bring about a better life, imagining that perhaps the Widow would soften her harsh ways. But right from the start, it was his wife who was in charge. She ridiculed him in front of others, and everything he did seemed wrong to her. After several years of marriage, the Widow was as much a virgin (if she ever had been) and as much a widow as the very first day.

In the village, they said that when her first husband died, the Widow made a cruel commitment. Because she could no longer be with the man she loved, she decided that she would never belong to another. She swore against remarriage. And what better way to achieve this than by marrying Uncle Rosendo, the village idiot?

With time, he got tired of being in the house with her, breathing in her dead husband's air. And so, with no children (because how could there be children?), he became a regular at the tavern.

He began to get drunk every afternoon, and, thanks to this, many repressed memories inside him were set free.

Some days, after Saladina was finished at Mr. Tenderlove's office, the Winterlings would pass by the tavern. Seeing them there, Uncle Rosendo would remember Don Reinaldo and talk of old times. He said, nostalgically, that their grandfather had been one of the best friends he had ever had and that the village had never been the same without him. Once he warmed up, there was no stopping him, and the Winterlings noticed how the others would barge in and tell him to shut up, nudge him in the ribs, or gesture at him to stop.

One day, he told them about how Don Reinaldo had cured a man of "his own childhood." The poor man couldn't stop saying "no." From the moment he got up until he went to sleep, he refused everything: his mother, his wife and kids, work, the wine they served him at the tavern, the rain, the flowers, and the sun. Don Reinaldo went to his house, took off his corduroy jacket, and got into bed with him. He spent the night there, sharing voices, nightmares, and sweat, and in the morning, the man felt much better.

"Oh, he was a fine man!" added Uncle Rosendo. "He didn't deserve what he got. He truly was everyone's doctor, until they accused him of being a witch doctor and a Bolshevik. He thought that wealth was poorly distributed and that it was a social injustice not to help the most needy. That was all. Don Reinaldo came out of prison all anxious; he felt persecuted by everyone. He never understood why they put him in there. The fear turned his mind. He started to do strange things . . . That's when . . . "

Suddenly, the innkeeper turned up the volume on the television.

". . . as I was saying," continued Uncle Rosendo, trying to make his voice heard over the TV announcer. "But that's when they gave poor Tristán a beating, too. I don't know . . . those gun-crazy folks came along shouting and shooting in the air. No one got away from them."

It wasn't quite seven o'clock, but after that comment, someone pulled him off his seat, bringing about his nightly tumble ahead of time.

Boom.

Shortly thereafter, slightly stooped, Meis's Widow jumped down from her wagon.

18

"I TOLD YOU QUITE CLEARLY on the first day not to eat garlic or onion, Saladina!" protested Mr. Tenderlove. "That's all I asked of you . . . "

Lately, the visits to the dental mechanic's office, which at the start were quite brief—just taking the time necessary to clear a spot, insert a tooth, fix it to the bone with cement, and stitch up the wound on the gum—had begun to grow longer. After the work was done, they stayed chatting in the office, and the conversation became more and more expressive and personal. Instead of real anesthetics, the dental mechanic used a local spirit distilled from herbs, and so when Saladina got up from the chair, she was a different woman altogether. Far from feeling pain or discomfort, her head would spin, and she felt pleasure and a swirling desire to dance.

They held similar views on many things, and Tenderlove, in addition to being kind and good with his hands, turned out to be quite a cultured man of the world. Saladina spoke to him of the time she and her sister had spent in England: what the people there were like, how they dressed, what they ate, and all the films they had seen. She told him that she never had to work there because she lived with her lover in a mansion, that she had been the lead actress in two films, and that the producers were falling over themselves to have her star in a third, but that she hadn't been able to take the role because the war broke out. He just watched her with his gray, penetrating eyes.

Saladina enjoyed that man's company; there was something hesitant and mysterious in his persona that made him interesting. For example, you could never get a definitive answer from him: "we'll see" or "you could say that" is all that he would say. In response to the direct question of how much it would cost her to fix up her teeth, he would answer with "Oh, not too much" or "As much as I said the other day."

One day, Saladina dared to ask him why he had never married. Through Uncle Rosendo, she had found out that the dental mechanic was very discreet in his private life and he didn't like to talk about it. Tenderlove told her that essentially there were things that were meant to be and things that weren't and there was no explanation for them at all. Why did ham go with turnip tops, while fish didn't go with cheese? *Fish with cheese?* It was this mad reasoning that was so attractive to gloomy Saladina.

Among his many other qualities, Tenderlove had a great sense of humor. On occasion, he would disappear from the office into the shadows of the house. After a moment, he would come back dressed up as a priest, a cabaret girl, a nun, or a soldier, but nearly always in dark, tight-fitting clothes that accentuated his enormous masculine bulge.

This was the game they played: Tenderlove would disappear, and Saladina had to guess what disguise he would put on. The dental mechanic was a great fan of clothing in general. Saladina had kept some very skimpy silk stockings that she bought years before in England. She wore them to his office specifically to attract his attention. When she told him that the women in England made their own underwear from the remains of gunned-down enemy pilots' parachutes, he was beside himself.

His participation in the Spanish Civil War was a thorny topic. He had been part of the underground resistance, the *maquis*—that motley collection of bearded fugitives who, from 1940 onward, had fought from their hideaways in the mountains of Galicia, living on blackberries, animal-bone broths, and water from streams. Saladina would casually mention the resistance, without imagining the rage he felt just hearing the word *maquis*. In fact, she *could* imagine it, thanks to Uncle Rosendo, but she still dragged it up. She was impressed at the thought of him belonging to such a virile and rebellious group of men. At any opportunity, she would ask him why he no longer went up the mountains to take food or blankets to his comrades.

Saladina would return to the house glowing, in an excellent mood, and Dolores, who was accustomed to her sister's vinegary disposition, was pleased but also worried to see her like that.

In fact, since her sister had started going to the dental mechanic's office, she had filled out and looked healthier. She got up at dawn, and, while she whistled childhood ditties from England to herself, she bustled to and fro throughout the house in great spirits, bursting with frenetic energy. No sooner had she built a new woodshed, she'd be mucking out the stable, the cow included, or watering the geraniums. Then she'd be cooking or heading down to the river to fish for trout.

But Dolores knew from experience (and this is why she wasn't quite convinced) that spells of good humor did not last long in her sister, usually giving way to dark and gloomy moods.

Until now, Saladina had never been in love. She didn't know how to give herself over to it. But she had her reasons: apart from Dolores, and perhaps, back in his day, her grandfather, no one had ever loved her. As a consequence, she had built a wall around herself without even a single fissure or attachment. She had learned that in England everyone did this and that it was, without a doubt, the most practical way to survive.

But now, having discovered the pleasure of feeling in love (because with time she was discovering that oh yes, she was madly in love with Mr. Tenderlove), she appeared self-confident and much more independent. What's more, she wanted to know if others felt the way she did.

One day, she asked the country teacher when she saw him on the road to the mountain.

"Uncle Rosendo, when you see your wife in the morning, do you feel butterflies in your stomach?" Uncle Rosendo replied that what he felt when he saw her were more likely moths.

Or she would ask Don Manuel, the priest.

"Father, you love God, don't you?"

"Of course, dear girl, what kind of nonsense is this?"

"And you don't stutter when you speak to Him? You don't blush or feel your insides churning?"

The priest walked off without answering.

She asked Tristán, who raised capons, when she saw him one day at the tavern.

"Do you get goose bumps when you see a woman you like?"

And when she got home, she would write a list of all the words associated with love: butterflies, moths, goose bumps, stuttering, lion's roar.

By this stage, she was an expert in lists, and she had all kinds of them: lists of friends and enemies, shopping lists, blacklists, to-do lists, lists of shoes she didn't have, lists of actors with and without an Oscar. It was as if her frightened and chaotic mind needed the absurd order these lists had to offer. Through these lists, she became who she wanted to be.

But that day in his office, Tenderlove didn't feel like talking and was quite surly. He was fixated on the fact that Saladina had eaten garlic or maybe onions.

"I swear on my mother that I didn't."

The dental mechanic, who at that moment was polishing a tooth, looked at her out of the corner of his eye. Saladina had flushed cheeks and feverish eyes. Because she had arrived by walking through the forest, her skirt had stirred up all kinds of butterflies and insects from the long grass, and now they were stuck in her hair like shiny bobby pins. She was breathing heavily.

"You did so! You ate something. I knew it as soon as I saw you, or, should I say, since I smelled you coming."

The dental mechanic started preparing the cement with a sour look on his face. Saladina watched him pensively. She thought that Tenderlove had a muscly face. She also thought that underneath all that tension he had hidden away lies and that when he smiled, his eyes didn't change at all. She struck up the courage to break the silence.

"It's because of the titanium, isn't it? Yesterday they were saying on the television in the tavern that it's running out. Don't worry, you'll find another material to make teeth with. Is one of my new teeth missing? I'm happy to wait . . . "

Tenderlove stared at her in silence. Some mosquitoes disentangled themselves from her hair and began to buzz around her head.

"It's not because of that. I have three teeth to go. But I'll get them. I'm just . . . I'm just waiting for the material to arrive . . . "

"Well, maybe it's because I haven't paid you yet, right, Tender? It's just that you haven't told me how much you're charging for the replacement!"

Tenderlove shifted abruptly, as if he'd been disturbed.

"How am I supposed to work with that rotten garlic you have in your mouth . . . You stink, Winterling!"

"Why do you talk to me like that? And why do you call me that? I have a name . . . "

Tenderlove looked at her. He slammed the dish with the cement in it on the table.

"The truth is that I don't know why I call you that. Sometimes the tongue is quicker than the word. Look, now that you're here I'll put in today's tooth, but you'll have to wait for the remaining three . . . "

And so that day Saladina was forced to hear, with a heavy heart, that she was not to come back until Tenderlove sent word.

19

AT DUSK, lulled by the *clack clack* of the Singer, more and more often Dolores felt a tingling in her spine. Now that they were settled in the village, and especially since her sister had become more independent, she had the feeling that something big was about to happen.

She didn't quite know what the feeling was. Sometimes she confused it with a sense of lacking.

Perhaps, she thought to herself, it was just women's nonsense.

Other times, however, she thought that whatever she was waiting for was already right there, along with her sister, Greta the cow, and her simple life, beneath the stars and the sky, in the house with the fig tree in Tierra de Chá.

The sun was coming up on a warm day when her feelings began to take shape. The earth gave off a damp smell, and the chimneys puffed out a dirty white smoke. The whole countryside resonated with the chirping of insects and the crackling of grass. The time had come to reap the corn and shear the sheep. Dolores went out to the orchard to feed the chickens. The kitchen window was open with the radio on. Just then, the announcer's voice interrupted the music with breaking news. News that would disrupt their whole routine. News that would destroy the monotonous safety the two sisters had been clinging to since their arrival. Ava Gardner, the famous American actress, "the most beautiful animal in the world," was coming to Spain to make a movie. Soon, she would be arriving in Tossa de Mar to shoot *Pandora and the Flying Dutchman*.

The announcer said it was great news, because the film would create jobs for many local people on the coast. "Ava Gardner is coming to Spain," the Winterling told the chickens.

She shrugged her shoulders and threw more breadcrumbs.

She didn't think of it again until nightfall.

Her sister came back from the tavern, and they took the animals up the mountain. She spent the afternoon sewing the hem of a dress, a commission that the Winterlings received every year from a certain family in Santiago. They went to the forest to gather kindling, made fig jam, listened to their soap opera, had dinner, and then got ready for bed.

But before she got into bed, while she was putting on her nightdress, Dolores felt a shiver run down her spine. A tingling like spiders ran through her bones and up her back, right into her head.

She didn't want to pay any attention to it.

But once she was lying down, she couldn't stop tossing and turning. She didn't get a wink of sleep. Finally, she sat on the edge of her sister's bed and watched her in the darkness. She thought that Saladina looked even more ugly asleep than awake.

"Hey, Sala," she whispered after a while, seeing that her eyes were open. "Do you know where Tossa de Mar is?"

Saladina, who had no idea at all about geography, took a while to answer.

"Where do you think it is, you dummy? By the sea, of course! You can tell from the name: Tossa de *Mar*."

They fell silent.

Dolores went back to her bed and covered herself in blankets.

Suddenly, Saladina woke up again.

"Tell me the truth," she squawked from her bed. "Why did you ask that question in the middle of the night?"

"There's nothing to tell," her sister responded fearfully from beneath the covers. "It just crossed my mind to ask you. Things pop into my mind, I have a brain, you know, I'm not a chicken . . . "

She lay in the darkness with her eyes open. The house was calm, and surges of heat wafted up from the open trapdoor. The smell of manure comforted her.

She could feel her heart thumping in her ears.

Greta Garbo the cow mooed languidly in the stable.

But that night, while they slept, a sea grew in the sisters' bedroom.

IT WAS A SEA that looked like the one Dolores had seen off the English coast, or off Coruña, or maybe even like the one in the port at Santander where they had been abandoned with their cardboard suitcases. But it was a strange sea, because the chickens scratched in it, and actors and actresses from Hollywood lived in it—Greta Garbo, Frank Sinatra with his powerful voice, skinny little Audrey Hepburn, and Clark Gable, the King of Hollywood.

Throughout the following days, Dolores heard it while she went about her daily chores—immense and powerful and ever nearer, turning her actual world into a narrow and boring place—an ocean pulling at her, calling her: "Did you hear that Ava Gardner is coming to Spain?"

To Spain?

Ava Gardner coming to Spaaaaaain?

Sometimes, the sea was like a cornfield, with waves that ebbed and flowed. Dolores was in the middle of it. It smelled of salt, and the smell impregnated her clothes, her hair.

Her head was full of sand, bubbles, and chickens. She fell asleep to this aroma and woke up hearing sighs in her own chest, the deep and heavy swell of the sea.

She was the sea.

EVER SINCE DOLORES had dropped the plate of feed while she was rescuing her sister, the chickens hadn't stopped pecking at the ground beneath the fig tree. They became troublesome. They stayed under there all day, and it had become a filthy pit of excrement, dirt, stones, feathers, and feed in which the chickens pecked even at each other, scrapping and scuffling fiercely among themselves.

A sense of violence, of strange and pointless aggression, hung in the air until, one day, they woke up to find that one of the chickens was dead. Since then, for some reason, none of the others had laid an egg.

They spoke about it in the tavern, and everyone recommended that they go and speak with Tristán, the rooster raiser, who was also quite good with chickens.

Tristán was a tall and taciturn man. He had a magnificent house, near the fountain with only one tap. He spent his days with his birds—still, silent, and solitary.

The rooms on the lower floor were entirely dedicated to the chickens that roosted there comfortably, with the air of landholders. On the upper floor, in a large room with walls so covered in filth you could hardly see the moldings or fixtures, the capons were locked in cages. Here, he fattened them up with dough to sell at market. Three times a day, at nine, three, and eight, Tristán would lumber up the staircase, open the cages, and stuff into their beaks a ball of ground wheat and corn dipped in water and white wine.

The younger capons needed softer balls of feed, and the older ones tended to shed their feathers, so Tristán was always kept busy. That's without even mentioning Christmas, when at least three or four times a day he had to get the capons drunk with a spot of cognac so that the meat would be tastier.

The capon is an awkward animal, stupid and quick-tempered, and there could be no doubt that some of this had rubbed off onto Tristán. What's more, due to living in such close quarters with these birds, he had begun to resemble them physically as well. He had the same cloudy eyes, the jowls, and long, sharp fingernails. Just like them, he was fat and unfit, with bruised skin and fine hair all over his body.

Tristán and his capons looked like they had hatched from the same egg.

Sitting by the cages all day long, either in silence in order to avoid spooking the animals, or playing music by Chopin to fatten them up, he began to develop odd habits. He became awkward and solitary. If the poor birds didn't swallow when he put the feed in their mouth, he'd beat and insult them. The terrified capons would keep their heads down and scurry off to a corner of the cage. So then Tristán would have to go in, on all fours, and pull them out. He'd put the dough back in their mouths, and they'd spit it out. Tristán would slap them and then start with the insults.

That's how he spent his life.

A lot of things were said about him: that he fed the capons cyanide, that he warded off the black dog of depression by drinking the cognac meant for the birds, and that he let his own mother die so he could cash in on an insurance policy and buy his house in Tierra de Chá. In fact, he'd inherited the obligation to tend to the bird business, and he'd never really liked it.

Gossip.

The Winterlings went to see him to explain their problem.

"Chickens are pretty clever, even though they're stupid," explained Tristán, without looking up, as he put a ball of bread dough in one of the capon's beaks. "They want you to know something. If they've been scratching at the ground there for days, it's not just for the spilled feed. Something is lurking beneath the fig tree that you don't know about."

He agreed to have a look at the chickens when he got an opportunity. His work barely gave him a chance to leave the place.

Once they got home, Dolores got out a broom and got to sweeping all around the fig tree. Barely five minutes had gone by before the broom hit something hard. The Winterling bent down to look. The ground had already been well turned over, so she barely had to dig at all. No, it wasn't a root, or a stone either. What was *that* doing there? Was it one of those treasures from Cuba that her grandfather had told her about on cold winter nights?

With the feeling that there was something important buried there, she pulled out a little hoe and called her sister.

The Winterlings squatted down to watch. They stayed there for a few minutes in silence, with their eyes fixed on the ground. They got back up again. They hugged, then got back down on the ground on their knees.

"For the love of God, let's see what's inside!" clamored one of them.

"I'm scared!" said the other, dancing on the spot.

"Me too."

Saladina bent down to dig with the hoe, but she soon stopped.

"We're disturbing the past," she said. "Do you think it's worth it, after all the sacrifices we made to be here? We've been here a while and still no one suspects a thing about our little secret . . . It's not worth it. Besides, whatever is in there doesn't belong to you."

"It's not yours either!"

The first sister jumped on the second one. She tried to grab hold of the hoe. But the second one struck back, pouncing on her like a panther. For a few minutes, they struggled like that on the ground. Finally, Saladina took control of the hoe and got back down on all fours. She shook the dust off herself. She was panting, her hair twisted and crazy, like snakes writhing over her eyes. She covered up what they had just found with dirt.

"Not a single word to anyone about this," she said almost breathlessly.

Dolores panted.

"Did you hear me?"

A FEW DAYS AFTER they had been digging under the fig tree, the whole town was turned upside down by the first in a series of events that were more or less linked together.

It all started when Ramón died in the Winterlings' stable. But it didn't occur to anybody that what happened that day was merely the beginning of everything that would follow. No one knew that things, like people and animals, yearn only for eternal repose and that it would have been better not to disturb the murky soil of the past.

Little Ramón had announced that he would return to Tierra de Chá, and he was true to his word. During his first visit on shore leave, he passed by the tavern. There he met Mr. Tenderlove, who was asking Don Manuel if Violeta da Cuqueira had come back down to the village.

"That witch?" asked the priest. "God help us . . . She would only come down here to prophesy someone's death."

Then the dental mechanic asked if the old lady from Bocelo had died yet.

"What do you mean is she dead yet? Good God!" complained the priest. "I told you already! I head up the mountain just to head back down again. I'm Sisyphus reincarnate! But instead of a rock, I've got holy oils. Condemned for the rest of my days . . . "

Tenderlove had no idea who Sisyphus was, and he didn't really care; he just shifted in his seat. He asked how old the lady was.

"At least a hundred," calculated the priest.

"Well..." answered Tenderlove. "Isn't it about time to administer something to that old Methuselah?"

The priest looked at him, horrified.

"No one goes until their time comes, and when the time comes, they go! Since when have you been so interested in little old ladies?"

But Tenderlove lowered his head, finished his wine in one gulp, wiped his mouth, and said not a word more.

That's how Little Ramón found out that the old lady from Bocelo was still around, a sack of skin and bones, telling everyone that soon she would have the piece of paper concerning the sale of her brain, which, according to her, was as magnificent as the Cathedral of Santiago. He also realized that each and every inhabitant of the village must have a contract of sale signed by Don Reinaldo.

He went about making some inquiries, and the next morning, before sunrise, he arrived at the Winterlings' house.

Dolores was alone. Saladina had woken with her mouth aflame. Since the evening before, her dentures had felt strange. She didn't eat, she devoured; she seemed as if overcome by a whirlwind that tore through food and made it disappear down her gullet, only to search for more.

There was no point sealing her lips shut, or asking her sister to take the chorizo and bread out of her sight. Her neck, arms, and body were enslaved to her mouth. If Saladina tried to keep it shut, she ran the risk of eating her tongue, and whenever her sister tried to intervene, she was bitten ferociously. Other times her mouth lay still, playing dead until suddenly, *snap*, it opened and closed, or she started cackling like a madwoman.

And so, despite the fact that Tenderlove had given her strict orders not to return to his office until he himself sent word, Saladina had no other option but to go there.

Without anyone inviting him in, Ramón opened the door, made a path through the chickens, and sat down on a bench. In the kitchen, the fire was roaring, and above it, in a pan, the breakfast was bubbling away. Among the strings of chorizo and blood sausages, wet shirts and underwear hung by the hearth to dry. The light of the fire reflected off the fire tongs and pan.

Looking around and smelling the odor of the house, Ramón felt a pang of nostalgia for the first time in many years. It was an odor in which he could distinguish the things he was made of. The smell of chorizo hanging by the hearth, an animal sleeping nearby in the stable, the bleach his mother used to clean the floors.

How much time had passed since he used to spend every afternoon here with his mother? Twenty-five years. But twenty-five years was nothing, because it felt like just yesterday that the women around the hearth were telling him jokes and stroking his hair, when his mother would unbutton her shirt and take out her breasts to feed him.

When he spoke about the people and the stories they would tell there in winter, his voice broke. Then, when he recalled how his mother had weaned him at the age of seven, he began to laugh. Unable to control himself, he covered his mouth with his hand, cackling with nervous and sometimes overwhelming laughter. He laughed, or he cried; as much as she watched him, Dolores couldn't figure out which.

Finally, Ramón wiped away the tears. He breathed in the smell again.

"He bought my mother's brain as well. That old hag hid the money, without telling me where, until the day she died. Tristán told me. But my mother was capable of anything . . ."

He tried to choke back a loud chortle that spooked a chicken. But the tears kept rolling down his cheeks.

Then, out of the blue and in a different tone, he began to talk about his friend Tomás, the fisherman of octopus and pout whiting from Ribeira.

"To tell the truth, it's been a long time since I've seen Tomás. At the Company, nobody's heard a word from him . . . He didn't even come to collect his wages. They're very surprised."

"Tomás?" Dolores stood up suddenly. She didn't know who Tomás was. They'd already told him they had only been in Ribeira a short time. "Too damp for the bones. We prefer Coruña, which is a real city, with streets, lamps, cars, shops where women's perfume and gentlemen's tobacco lingers in the air. But now we're here: werewolves, ghosts, and lost souls. That has its charm as well. Would you care for a drink?"

"Milk," declared Little Ramón pointedly, as if he'd already prepared his answer.

"Milk," said Dolores, bumping into his legs as she turned around, her arms stiff in the air, looking from side to side. "Righto then . . . "

Just then she heard singing in the distance, a voice that for the moment was still unidentifiable yet familiar, coming in from the orchard. She looked through the window and saw Mr. Tenderlove carrying a huge sack on his back. She looked closer: that huge sack was, in fact, the monstrosity that was her sister.

What was Saladina doing riding Tenderlove's hump like that, singing and cackling like a madwoman?

Opening the door, Tenderlove disposed of his cargo abruptly. Saladina fell to the floor without missing a word of "Ten Green Bottles," laughing in fits and starts with bits of snot blowing out her nose.

"What have you done to my sister?" asked Dolores, horrified.

The dental mechanic explained timidly that he'd done nothing out of the ordinary: he just gave her a bit of brandy as an anesthetic. It turns out Saladina hadn't had any breakfast and so . . .

"You quack! You shouldn't be fixing people's mouths!" screeched Dolores in a rage. "You're not qualified!"

"Qualified, whoop-whoop!" began Saladina from the floor, rolling over with laughter. "Quaaaaalifiiiiieeed, whoop-Tender-green, green bottles, bada-whoop-qualified hanging on the wall!"

Dolores dismissed the dental mechanic, who, put out by such a slight, lit out for the main road as fast as he could, slightly stooped over. Then she helped her sister get into bed. Saladina went upstairs without missing a beat in her song, whoop-Tenderlove-bada-whoop qualifieeeeeed.

Once she had laid her sister down, the Winterling set about attending to—or rather, getting rid of—Ramón, who had been greatly amused by the spectacle and was still waiting for his glass of milk.

The Winterling explained that there wasn't any milk because the cow hadn't been milked yet; in fact, it was high time to do that but between one thing and the other, she hadn't been able to do it. Jesus, couldn't he hear her mooing? No, Ramón couldn't hear it. Well, just when you arrived, I was getting ready to milk her. There's no milk, but I can offer you anise. Dolores hurried to explain that a doctor in Coruña had prescribed anise to cure Saladina from a bout of flatulence, and what do you know, she took a liking to the remedy and now is something of a drinker. So you see . . . But Ramón wasn't laughing. He was lost in thought.

"I want the piece of paper," he said suddenly. "You might as well go and get it because that's what I came here for."

He got up quickly and said that while she looked for the contract from the sale of the brain, he'd milk the cow himself and it would bring back fond memories.

It was early, one of those bright mornings close to summer. Smoke over the tiled roofs. The pealing of bells. Lately, there had been heavy storms that had forced them to stay indoors. But that day, all was calm in the countryside. The sun had that brilliance that shines through after a storm, when the air is clean and fresh. From time to time, they could hear Saladina singing and sobbing, although more and more faintly each time. Finally, she seemed to have fallen asleep.

Through the window, Dolores saw Ramón rummaging around in the shed. Among the rusty plow and the other farm tools, he was searching for something. She saw him go back into the stable, the milk pail clinking against his leg.

As children, before the outbreak of the war, the Winterlings and Little Ramón had been playmates. Even though he was a few years younger, they would go together to the forest to look for gentian and ladybirds. They teased the donkeys by pulling their tails and swam together in the river. In winter, when it was very cold, they liked to go into the stables in the village, especially the very big ones, and lie down among the cows. The three of them needed warmth, and the cows gave it to them. Sometimes they lay among the cows until dawn broke.

Little Ramón's mother, Esperanza (Hope at Nicolasa's Door), had been their grandfather's maid. She hadn't found work since Don Reinaldo disappeared, and she lived off charity from the villagers and selling shawls she crocheted at the markets and festivals. Her son had grown up with barely any education, and when he turned sixteen, he went off to Coruña and sailed away on the first ship that offered him work.

Little Ramón went into the stable, and the Winterling went upstairs to see how her sister was doing. Saladina wasn't asleep, but she had calmed down, so Dolores decided to explain to her that they had a visitor in the house, Ramón, Little Ramón, and that right now he was in the stable trying to milk the cow.

"I was sure he was going to kiss me when he was carrying me like that, and I was holding very still and close to him, my breasts on his back . . . I was paralyzed, Dolores! I didn't want to move a muscle so that we could both take in that moment," said Saladina, clutching at the covers.

Dolores looked at her in desperation.

"What are you going on about, you idiot! You're drunk! I don't want to hear one more word about that quack. Didn't I tell you Ramón is here in the house?"

Saladina was silent. Suddenly, she appeared to emerge from her trance and jumped out of bed.

"Little Ramón is here? In our house?"

The window was open, and the fresh morning breeze blew in. In the distance, bent over the earth, a group of women worked in the fields. They broke the earth and slashed the grass with their mattocks. The breeze transported the smell of gorse and manure piled up to make fertilizer. A murder of crows slowly crossed the sky.

They opened the trapdoor. Straight away, the rancid smell of cow dung floated up at them. Down there was Ramón—they could see him, but he couldn't see them—looking for the perfect place to sit down. Finally, he placed the stool down next to the cow. The Winterlings let out a sigh of relief when they saw that all he wanted to do was milk the cow. Greta had woken up; she lifted her neck up to the sky and stared straight ahead, her mouth half-open and her eyes drooping as if she were confronted by ancient memories, blowing white breath out of her nostrils.

Many people in the village said that Esperanza, Little Ramón's mother, had died a suspicious death. They said that Don Reinaldo, who had employed her as a servant, had something to do with it . . .

That's not how it happened. Or at least, Little Ramón had no memory of the Winterlings' grandfather being involved in her death. Esperanza (Hope at Nicolasa's Door) died on a May morning, while making a five-needle crochet on the couch in her house. The kid, who was eating a sandwich and sitting right in front of her, saw how his mother's hands started trembling and her needlework fell to the floor. A spasm shook her entire body and then stopped, leaving an ironic smirk on her face. Ramón sat there with his eyes popping out of his head, his teeth clamped down on the bread, trying to work out if the expression on her face was glee or terror. His whole life had been like that: an eternal confusion of caresses and clips over the ear, laughter and crying, love and violence.

"Stop looking at me like that!" he finally exploded. He finished eating his sandwich and got up. He left the house convinced that his mother was dead, but he never knew if she had died of happiness or sadness. A few hours earlier, he had announced that he would be going to sea and would be away for two years, fishing the waters of Argentina.

Little Ramón let go of the cow's udders. He couldn't get comfortable on the stool, because its legs were bumping against the gorse branches. He picked it up and put it back down again.

"He suspects something," said one Winterling.

"Shut your mouth!" said the other, and slammed the trapdoor shut. They began to fidget, like they always did when they were nervous.

"I'm going down there!"

"Don't go down there, for the love of God!"

"I'm going!"

They opened the trapdoor again. One of the sisters climbed over the other one's rump, and they both sat down to watch. Ramón was milking the cow.

They closed the trapdoor, and Dolores went down to the stable as quickly as she could. Ramón heard a noise and turned around. When he saw the Winterling he gave a start, stood up, and took a few steps back.

"So you like milk," she said, looking at him fiercely.

But Ramón didn't answer. The Winterling's eyes radiated a strange light that kept him still. In those eyes, Ramón seemed to see tables and chairs, women falling, his mother making crochet in a frosty landscape, a cold February morning.

At that moment, Greta mooed languidly. She shifted and suddenly kicked out at Ramón, a single blow, right in the neck. He fell to the ground mumbling incomprehensible words about the Company and his friend Tomás.

The other Winterling, who had watched the whole scene from above, came down as well. Between the two of them, they tidied up the gorse branches and started to attend to Ramón. They grabbed a foot each and dragged him upstairs to the bedroom. They put him down on the bed and called the priest, explaining what had happened.

As was normal in such cases, the whole village came along with the priest. But the damage had been done, and by the next day, the young man was coughing up blood.

Eight days later, he was dead.

PART II

Perhaps only one winter remains for us.

HORACE,
"CARPE DIEM"

1

AS A MATTER OF PRINCIPLE, the nasty business about Ramón was never spoken of again. These things happen—accidents, tragedies. He certainly was very young, not even thirty years old, but life is full of surprises.

This all changed one afternoon when the mayor of Sanclás, the parish to which the village belonged, arrived at the Winterlings' house accompanied by the priest. He came to tell them that a judge in Coruña wished to speak with them.

They didn't much feel like talking about anything that a judge would be interested in, so they told the mayor and the priest that they'd go sometime soon. For now, they had sick chickens to care for. They wouldn't stop fighting, and it had been some time since any of them had laid an egg. It was something that required immediate attention.

When the mayor left, the priest hung around to speak with them. Between implications and insinuations, he let them know that things were about to get ugly. Now there was a judge involved, and now he, too . . . he, too, wanted the contract for the purchase of his brain. He also said that he hadn't mentioned anything to the judge, but that while he was administering the last rites to Little Ramón, he had mumbled something about a certain Tomás. Did they know who Tomás was?

No, the Winterlings hadn't the slightest idea who Tomás was.

Finally, Don Manuel pulled the door open. He said he'd come back later for the contract, seeing as it was just about lunchtime, and that they should have it ready for him.

"Woolly bear caterpillar, *vai cajar*," hummed the Winterlings in unison, their eyes on the door, when he was already outside.

Then Dolores put on her shawl, telling her sister that she was going to the tavern to see if she could find Tristán. "Are you coming?"

"I have things to do," answered Saladina, without further explanation.

Dolores looked at her in surprise.

"Things?"

"Things," replied her sister with an air of mystery, moving toward the kitchen.

"And what exactly do you need to do, if I may ask?"

"Things," repeated Saladina from the kitchen, where she was putting figs in a basket.

Dolores began to lose patience. She looked at the figs.

"What are you doing with those? You know they always upset your stomach . . ."

But Saladina didn't answer. She began peeling the figs and putting them in a pot with water. Then she got out the canister of sugar, took the lid off, and began to throw in handfuls. She was singing to herself.

"We already have enough fig jam," said Dolores.

The other Winterling continued what she was doing without responding. Finally, after stirring the figs and the sugar in the pot for a good spell, singing happily all the while, she turned around to address her sister, who was still standing there with her hands on her hips.

"The jam isn't for you or even for me. There are more people than us in the world, you know."

And so, Dolores ended up going to the tavern alone. Alone and confused.

But the rooster raiser wasn't alone; he was downing wine with a big group of people who were watching the door, waiting for Uncle Rosendo to arrive. As they told her, it was the big day: the country teacher had gone to Coruña to face his "moment of truth."

"His 'moment of truth'?" asked Dolores.

"His moment of truth," they responded, without taking their eyes off the door.

Besides the theories he had about the labyrinths of his wife's mind, Uncle Rosendo had many other philosophies he would expound in the tavern. For example, there was the theory that one is the exact opposite of what one purports to be: that is, if someone were to insist that they were shy, they would clearly be outgoing, and if someone tries to convince us that they are wise, then they know little, or, more likely, nothing. He also held to the theory that toothaches always began on Friday nights, and that the "pure and simple truth" is rarely pure and never simple.

He told the priest that in the beginning there was not the Word but the Lie and that the Lie often holds more truth than the truth itself.

But his million-dollar theory was the one about fate. The life and fate of every man, he said, comes down to a single moment.

This moment could pop up unexpectedly, like a toothache, for example (although not necessarily on a Friday afternoon), but when that moment presents itself, either you give yourself over entirely to it, or it never presents itself again.

His moment finally arrived the day he had to pass the exam to get certified as a country teacher. In truth, he'd never felt like gaining an official qualification, given that nobody in Tierra de Chá disputed his role as teacher, but he accepted the opportunity with the resignation used to accept unavoidable tasks. He put up a sign on the school that said "Closed by Formal Obligation," and hunkered down in the house to prepare.

For many days, he was nervous, but the week before the test was a nightmare. He prepared for that exam like his life depended on it. At the tavern in the evenings, he told everyone he was constantly studying with books, although Meis's Widow revealed that this was not true; he spent his day overwhelmed, staring out the window. Lately, all people could ask him about was the exam. They said they had no doubt he would pass, and patted him on the shoulder. These signs of affection made his stomach churn.

Finally, the day arrived.

It was the day they'd been waiting for.

The Winterlings had seen him going, very early in the morning, toward the square to catch the bus, wrapped in a corduroy jacket and a clean shirt with a stiff collar, breathing heavily. "There goes the teacher," they said to each other while they threw feed to the chickens. "Yes, there he goes."

Throughout the whole day, the entire town had been gathering to wait for him. And just a little after Dolores arrived at the tavern, he came down cautiously along the road.

"Here he comes!" yelled someone standing by the door of the tavern. Everyone rushed surreptitiously to the bar, and a ring of attentive listeners formed around it. Hanging on the results of the exam was the future of their children's teacher and the school in Tierra de Chá. But it was more than that. In fact, having a teacher and a school was the least important part.

"It all turned out for the best!" yelled a very serious Rosendo to the gathered listeners, as he pulled at the shirt button constricting his neck.

The townsfolk let out a sigh of relief.

"Thank goodness! And what did they ask you?"

"First allow your teacher something to drink," he said with affected restraint. "I'm as dry as a bone."

They put a glass of wine on the bar. Uncle Rosendo knocked it back in one gulp. The others looked at him expectantly.

"Well, they asked me," he said after burping, "if you buy three pine trees for one peso each, how much does it cost? That sort of thing, you know."

"Yes, yes, we know, three pesos! Easy! And what else?"

Uncle Rosendo became very serious. He gestured for more wine with one hand.

"Well, after that," he continued, stroking his chin, "it was a difficult exam, I'm not going to lie to you. Next, they asked me what elements might constitute a forest. And I answered 'trees' or 'wild beasts.'"

The men in the tavern burst into applause. They howled with pleasure and celebrated his response, toasting it with their glasses of wine. They were truly proud of everything their country teacher knew.

"Well said, Uncle Rosendo, well done! And what else did they ask you?"

"Next they asked me how much is seven by seven."

"And?"

"Well, here I didn't realize we'd gone back to mathematics, I thought we were still on geography, and my answer was the Miño River."

There was a general silence. A fly landed on the teacher's nose. He opened his palm, caught it, and pulled one of its wings off.

"So of course, I put my foot in it there . . ."

He let the fly go. Everyone watched it walk along the counter. Because it couldn't fly, it skittered from side to side.

"But at least you passed?"

Uncle Rosendo hiccupped twice.

"I passed."

Despite the general excitement and all the toasting on account of the teacher's story, Dolores managed to pull Tristán aside to talk. As was usual, the rooster raiser was in a hurry ("I have to get home much earlier than you can imagine"), but she managed to convince him to come by and have a look at the chickens.

And so, in the middle of the afternoon the next day, Tristán arrived at the house just as he had promised, followed by one of his capons and a rooster with white legs. As he explained, he was short on time because he had to take the rooster to Arzúa to sell it, and the capon was with him because it was still very young and would need to be fed soon.

First off, he wanted to ask some questions about the business at hand.

"Are they cantankerous, your chickens?" he asked.

The Winterlings said yes, that when they tried to shoo them out of the corner to feed and water them, they were irritable and wouldn't move.

Next Tristán asked if there was a rooster in the yard. The Winterlings replied that they had introduced a rooster a short time ago, but that the local *piñeira* chickens had been broody since the dawn of time and always laid eggs without the intervention of any rooster.

Tristán started nodding again as he looked at his watch.

"How long has this rooster been in the yard?" he asked.

The rooster must have been among the group for a few weeks, because Dolores had bought him more or less when Saladina began going to Tenderlove's office. Saladina smiled, showing the gaps in her gums. They also told him that since this rooster had come along, the other chickens had lost the habit of cleanliness. The worst was the poop all over the place.

The rooster raiser went into the yard and observed the chickens; he went to and fro, hunched over, clucking and crowing so as not to disturb them. He felt them from head to tail, examining their beaks, crests, wings, and feet. He could tell by touch if there was anything out of place, any damaged feathers or crests, and he touched their bellies and guessed, correctly, what they had eaten. It looked like he felt good in there, as if he were in his element. But then he looked at his watch again ("I have to get home much earlier than you can imagine") and said with alarm that he had to get going.

On the main road, on the way to the market at Arzúa, he came across the priest, flat on his face. Don Manuel was in a terrible mood, on his way back from asking the Winterlings for the contract for the sale of his brain, which they appeared to have forgotten. They made up a thousand excuses: the chickens, their sewing, the curd cheese . . . and what's more, they said they had no idea about the whole thing!

The priest had told them that he would be returning, that they would need to speak calmly about many things. He'd also told them that if they were thinking about going to the seven o'clock Mass, they shouldn't bother, because he wasn't feeling at all well. While he was walking down the road, he felt such heaviness in his head that it kept pulling him forward and eventually dragged him to the ground. Surely, it was some kind of flu.

"Answer me this," said Dolores, once they were alone again.

"What?" answered her sister.

"Do you think that woolly caterpillar suspects something?"

Saladina went over to the cupboard and took out the box of odds and ends.

"The priest?"

"The priest."

"About our little secret, you mean?"

"Yes, about our little secret."

But Saladina didn't answer. Once again, she seemed to be in another place. She picked out some blue flannel, wondering out loud about the jacket she was making. It'll look good with this material, won't it? And where are my glasses, Dólor? Ah, here they are, how silly of me. She got out the spool, sucked on the end of the cotton a couple of times, and threaded it.

2

JULY DRAGGED ON ENDLESSLY in the sticky humidity of Tierra de Chá. The bats flew low, drunk on heat and lust, the meadows glowed yellow, and the cicadas sang. The flies sought shelter in the houses, and bugs stuck to the skin.

Greta the cow mooed at five in the morning.

Saladina opened an eye, pulled an arm out from under the sheets, and, moved by a habit acquired over many years, felt the nightstand for her dentures. Then she said to herself, "You idiot, you don't have them anymore!" She got up. She dragged the porcelain chamber pot out from under the bed and put it in the middle of the room. She lifted up her nightdress, bent her knees, stuck her bottom out ceremoniously, and prepared to relieve herself. As the first jet hit the porcelain, she let out a large sigh.

The sound woke Dolores, who stayed in the fetal position, pretending to be asleep or dead, her gaze fixed on the leaky roof, an elephant, a star, a flower. The light was streaming into the bedroom, and for a while she stayed like that, intently watching the details and delicate movements that the damp had left on the whitewashed walls. Resting her ear on the pillow, she amused herself by counting her heartbeats. Another day. Another day in the company of her sister. The cow, the mountain, the Singer. Mending, sweeping, pulling down the cobwebs, and scrubbing. The same thing she did yesterday and will do tomorrow. For a while now, she had begun to think that the routine that had offered them so much consolation upon their arrival in Tierra de Chá was now nothing more than a way to grow old.

While she listened to the numbing stream of urine coming from her sister, she began to think about the movies, and the movies made her think of Ava Gardner. She could already begin to smell the sour, dreadful urine vapors, but she couldn't get the idea out of her head of Ava Gardner coming to Spain to make a movie. For that film, they'd be looking for body doubles, tall women with wavy hair who could speak English. She was thinking about what a good double she would be, when her sister's urine splashed her in the face. Why did she have to put up with this life? She covered herself with the sheets and turned over. Her sister clicked her tongue and moaned with pleasure as she inspected, between her open legs, the abundant foam that floated on top of her urine. She had finally finished.

Since she had heard the news, that afternoon in June when she was feeding the chickens, Dolores had not stopped thinking about how being an actress was what she had always wanted and that the film they were shooting on the Spanish coast was her opportunity. Again came the stream, like an open floodgate, Niagara Falls. Hadn't she finished already?

She was splashed again, this time on the shoulders. How disgusting. Would Saladina be on the pot all morning long?

Under the pretense of having to milk the cow, Dolores got up and went to the stable. Greta was in the corner, breathing calmly. Sitting on a stool, with her face to one side, Dolores rested her right cheek against the cow's flank. The cow had lost so much weight lately that her ribs were sticking out like the side of a galley, and you could surmise from her steely gaze that she was sick. To account for this thinness, the Winterlings had worked through thousands of possible excuses. Perhaps she was too old, perhaps going up and down the mountain had been too much exercise . . . But there was some other reason; strange things were going on in the village, and Greta was a victim, too.

It wasn't just the village. Something had turned in the universe in which the two women had comfortably lived up until that point. Signs of a secret domestic tension were floating in the air. Gone were the childish, innocent affairs of days gone by. They lived together, worked together, and slept together like a pair of friends who don't really know each other, increasingly aware that something was coming between them. Between the comings and goings to the mountain, the arguments and the moments of warmth, discontent was taking seed in the two women's hearts. For some time, the universe had been turning—but now it was *twisting*.

Every day, Dolores asked at the tavern if anyone knew the exact date that Ava Gardner was supposed to arrive in Spain. Nothing. Nobody knew a thing about it. They didn't even know who Ava Gardner was. Then one day, Dolores went up to the bar for a jug of wine, and the mistress of the house, who always watched the television, said that on the newsreel they'd announced that an American actress had left New York and was currently at a hotel in London, preparing to come to Spain. Was that the actress she'd been asking about the other day?

When she got home, Dolores found Saladina eating figs in the kitchen. She was still waiting for Tenderlove to call her, to put in the remaining teeth. She hadn't seen him since that day that he had brought her home drunk, so she still had three empty spots in her gums. That morning, making the most of the fact that her sister had gone to the tavern, she had put two jars of homemade jam in a basket, along with a few figs and the flannel jacket that she'd just finished. With the basket on her head, she went off to Mr. Tenderlove's house.

But the dental mechanic wouldn't even open the door. He limited himself to yelling at her from the window that he didn't have her teeth yet, that he'd call her.

"Can I come in for a bit, Tender?" she asked timidly. "I've got some presents for you."

"I'm very busy," came his reply. And then he shut the window.

Saladina went back home with the basket on her head and entered the kitchen. She was sitting there, eating figs mindlessly, when her sister walked in. She picked them out of the basket, pulled off the stalks with her gums, and spat them on the floor. Then she put them in her mouth whole and swallowed them, barely chewing.

Her sister watched them travel down her gullet—

Gulp.

And then the lumps disappeared.

Saladina didn't even look up when Dolores entered. She had been waiting for her, but while she was doing so, she began to feel sick. She felt alone and abandoned, feeling absence like a bolt through the heart.

"They've been like that for a while," said Saladina, staring ahead with a fig in her mouth.

Dolores looked at her without understanding.

"Who?" she asked, looking around.

But Saladina didn't reply; she just spat the stalk out onto the ground.

Alarmed, Dolores uncovered the Singer, threaded a spool of cotton, and sat down to finish a job. For a while all that could be heard was the monotonous *clack, clack* of the sewing machine.

It began to rain outside.

A tawny owl flew over the house.

Saladina got up and went over to the window.

"All they ask for is a few words of comfort, perhaps a bit of company," she said.

Her sister held up the dress she was sewing . . . yes, she'd been working on it for a while, the bust, and the armpit . . . soon it would be finished. She stopped the machine and glanced around. She realized that during her absence, her sister had not only been eating figs, but she'd emptied the entire bottle of anise.

"Who are you talking about?" she asked. "I tell you, sometimes you drive me crazy."

"I'm talking about them," said Saladina, pointing to the chicken yard with a trembling finger.

Her sister looked outside.

"The chickens?" she asked. "They're doing better now. I already told you that yesterday one of them laid an egg. It seems Tristán cured them just with his presence."

Saladina sat down again.

"My guts are churning," she said.

"Here we go again, the same old story about your guts. It's because of the figs," her sister told her, starting up the machine again. "You've been eating figs for months. You'll get the runs. Should I make you a chamomile tea?"

"Remember to dig a nice deep hole when I die, Dolores . . . "

Dolores kept sewing, wrapped up in the deafening noise of the machine. Finally, she spoke: "You farted."

"And if I die sitting down, first lay me out on the bed, like we did with Little Ramón and also with . . . "

Suddenly, and brutally, Saladina grabbed her sister by the wrist.

"And didn't we do the same with your Tomás?" she asked with a fierce glance.

Dolores disengaged her wrist and stopped the Singer. Ever since she had gotten up that morning, she had tried to contain herself, but she couldn't do it any longer. That last comment was too much. She pushed her sister aside, went upstairs, and shut herself in the bedroom.

From underneath the bed, she pulled out her suitcase and began to fill it with clothes. She pulled down the portrait of Clark Gable and wrapped it up in a nightdress. Get out of here. That's what she'd do. Because in the end, what tied her to her sister? Why did she have to live with her forever? Not all sisters lived together. Tossa de Mar—just saying those words out loud filled her mind with salt and freedom. She already had everything she needed in her suitcase when she heard footsteps in the hallway. The door opened slowly, as if pushed by a breeze.

Saladina stood in the doorway with the lantern in her hand. She was staring at Dolores with tired eyes, full of anger like black flashes.

Then she began to speak. Or rather, to spit words out. Her sentences came out concisely, heavy and scathing, throwing the memories in her sister's face, the terrible guilt for everything that happened in those few days.

But even more than guilt, what she felt was numbness, a hollow fear inside of her. Fear in the form of a frozen, slimy hole where there was once security in the earlier days. The days before her wedding. The days before they fled.

It was 1942. Dolores had just married a certain Tomás, fisherman of octopus and pout whiting. It was a simple wedding: a cream dress that went below the knee, a bouquet of heather, a supper of hot chocolate and churros. She had been in her new home for a week when she began to realize that every morning when she saw her husband, she felt a strange twisting in her stomach, a dull ache.

What was she doing with this man who burped as he ate breakfast hunched over the table, not saying a single word? What was she doing with this brute who stank of fish?

No matter how much she thought about it, she couldn't understand why she'd decided to get married. She had been educated and brought up well, had acted in a movie, and even spoke English. She must have confused marriage with something else. Then she remembered her sister's warnings: "Shortly after men get married, they develop bad habits, they grow a gut, they stink of farts . . . "

And so one day she told him, "Look, Tomás, my sister is ill. I'm going to Coruña for a few days to look after her."

Standing next to her just-packed suitcase, listening to the words her sister spat out, Dolores recalled how Tomás had shifted in his seat, raised his head, and looked at her. She remembered how his black eyes locked on her, and she remembered his words.

"You're not going anywhere."

"It's only for a few days," she replied.

"I've heard that little story before," he said, still staring at her.

"It's no story. My sister is ill."

"And what's wrong with that toothless freak?"

"A bit of respect!"

Dolores remembered (and Saladina told her) how, finally, Tomás had allowed her to leave. And her sister reminded her of his words at the door: "One month, Dolores. If you're not back after one month, I'm going to find you and bring you back, dead or alive."

While she got the clothes back out and put away the suitcase, Dolores remembered that she did go back.

But not alone: her sister Saladina went with her.

3

"I KEEP TELLING YOU—you go around all day obsessed with that *Superstars* magazine and the sea. What is this I keep hearing you say in your sleep about Ava Gardner?" Saladina asked her sister. "Does it have anything to do with the suitcase you packed the other day?"

They had been baking bread in the communal oven. The communal stone oven was a meeting place for all the villagers in Tierra de Chá, especially for the women who didn't go to the tavern. While they built up the fire at six in the morning, throwing on dry gorse branches, they solved the world's problems. Meis's Widow would spend her entire day there, whether she had to bake bread or not. That was where she could speak openly about her *absence*, explaining to everyone that it was like an intense burning in the kidneys that struck at sundown, or like something that dwelt in the hereafter, beyond the walls of her house. She was the one who spread the news that Saladina was having new teeth installed at Tenderlove's office, as well as the news that she had fallen in love with the dental mechanic. It was also through Meis's Widow that they heard, around the oven, about the death of Ramón under strange circumstances, and that a judge from Coruña required a statement from the Winterlings.

But for now they were alone. With a wooden spatula, they had scraped the ash from the oven while the heat flushed their cheeks red.

With all her sister's nagging, Dolores had no option but to confess. In the tavern, the news had been confirmed: Ava Gardner was about to arrive in Spain to film a new movie. Do you remember? We

136

read about it in *Superstars*. For the shooting in Tossa de Mar they need body doubles, tall women with dark and wavy hair, who speak English if possible, for certain ensemble scenes so that the actress can take a break.

Hearing this, Saladina was so shocked that she couldn't speak. With trembling hands, she began to sprinkle the flour on the dough, and then, using a large peel, flat and round, she pushed it into the back of the oven. She sealed the oven with cow manure, then turned slowly back to her sister, still trembling.

"No, no, no . . . you're not thinking of going there and applying to be . . . a double?"

A *double*. There are beautiful words, and then there are ugly words. Hard words and soft words. Friendly words and hostile words. Flabby ones and muscly ones. Saladina had lists and lists of words. They both knew the word "double" from their *Superstars of Cinema* magazine. But while that word transported one Winterling to an exotic location, it left the other one face to face with misery.

Dolores wiped her hands nervously on her apron and said that perhaps she would, why not?

"All the men in the village find me attractive," she added. "They whistle at me every time we walk across the square. It would just be for a scene or two. That is, if they take me at all."

Saladina dropped the peel to the ground. A wave of rage rose within her.

"It's always the nude scenes that the actresses refuse to do! You filthy pig!"

"Well, it's not always like that . . . " Dolores went quiet, then prepared herself. "I've been waiting for years, half my life, for this chance. I don't know what it will be like, but I live for it, it's what I'm chasing . . . It gets me through the day, Saladina, it makes me climb the mountain, scrub, sew, tend to the animals. I can't think of anything else and . . . who knows . . . something's going on in the village. Maybe we only have a short amount of time left. Perhaps only one winter remains for us. Perhaps tomorrow will be too late. I have to—"

"You have to leave? The men whistle at you? Let me tell you something, you dummy, you're gushing like a thirteen-year-old girl, repeating nonsense you've read in *Superstars*. You can't ever change your life. No matter how far you travel, or what you seek abroad, your life will continue to be what it is. It's the life you have now. The life that lives *inside of you*."

Dolores dismissed her by reminding her that lately she, too, had wanted to change her life, with her new dentures. And that she had noticed that she was getting on well with Mr. Tenderlove, and that . . .

"Who do you think you are, Ava Gardner?" snorted Saladina. "And anyway, what you're talking about costs money! We don't even have enough to pay for my teeth. Look me in the eye if you dare! I'm missing three teeth! You think I'm getting them to show off?"

Dolores looked at her sister. With her mouth open, teeth missing, she truly was repulsive.

Her head down, Dolores began to decorate the rest of the dough by covering it with hard-boiled eggs. Her eyes began to water.

"It looks like one of the sheep is pregnant. We can make lots of curd cheese and sell it . . . I believe—I'm convinced that I found out about Ava Gardner coming to Spain for a reason. Fate is guiding me to this path!" She began to sob. "If . . . if I was standing there feeding the chickens when the news came on the radio, it was for a reason . . . I don't normally feed them at that time."

Saladina grabbed a lock of Dolores's hair, pulled her toward her, and stared at her fixedly.

"There are two worlds, Dolores: the one you see through your eyes and the one you see through the camera. Only the first one is real. In the movies, everything has its reason. If Ashley ends up married to Melania, a good and adorable woman, it's for a reason. But life is different. It's full of stupid events and stupid days that don't mean a thing. Things *are* and that's just it; you have to accept it and move on. Anyway, you wouldn't want to be like Ava Gardner. Didn't you know she divorced Mickey Rooney?"

Her sister rebutted her between sobs.

"Yes, because she was looking for tenderness, friendship, and understanding in him. I read about it in *Superstars*. But he would leave her in bed and go out to play golf. Just like my Tomás . . . "

"Your Tomás never played golf."

"No, but he did go out to fish for octopus, which is kind of the same."

Saladina got even closer.

"Now that you mention octopus . . . "

Dolores twisted her neck away. The putrid stench of her sister's half-finished mouth crawled over her.

"You know why I'm talking about octopuses. Only I know what you did . . . "

"You're right, Sala." The tears were streaming down Dolores's cheeks. "Don't think I don't remember that. Do you think . . . Well, I think . . . I think about it constantly, I'm obsessed. Do you think that I . . . that *we* did the right thing, Sala?"

Saladina looked at her fingernails, all covered in flour.

"Such as things were, *you* did what you had to do."

Dolores forced a smile.

"*We* did, didn't we?"

"Fine, *we* did. Happy now?" Saladina rolled her eyes.

This time, Dolores expressed herself clearly.

"You're not suggesting that I have to take sole responsibility for it, are you?"

"Oh, no!" Saladina smiled to herself. "But I'm not going to either; that's the last thing I need!"

Dolores looked at her for a moment, with a brutal desire to insult her.

"Don't play with fire," Saladina warned.

"You're ruining my dreams . . . "

"I'm not ruining them for you, Dolores. You forged your own destiny. We did, or rather, *you* did what you had to do, but now you can't just wander off into the wide world like that, let me tell you. You have to be responsible," Saladina went on distractedly. "Where did you say they're doing it?"

"Doing what?"

"The filming . . . "

"In Tossa."

"Ah yes, Tossa de Mar! When one makes a decision of this caliber, one must commit to the consequences. We spent a whole night making a plan, and I said about a thousand times that you shouldn't marry that fisherman. Would it be far?"

"Would what be far?"

"Tossa."

The tears were flowing for Dolores. Round and brilliant, they rolled down her dress.

"Somewhere in Catalonia."

They gathered up the flour that was left on the worktop and put away the peel.

Saladina became pensive again. Her blood was boiling like poison.

4

THE NEXT DAY, they went up Bocelo Mountain to take the old lady some of the bread they had made. For a while now, they had been worried that Tenderlove wouldn't put the remaining teeth in Saladina's mouth until he was paid, and, according to everyone in the village, the old lady had bundles of money, hidden under her mattress.

They found the old lady sitting in her hut, cooking a sausage over the fire. She didn't look like she was a hundred years old. In fact, she looked like she existed outside of time. When she saw them, she let them in and sat them down. She said that she'd never felt better in her life, now that she thought that her time had come.

The Winterlings got right down to it. They'd brought her a few crusts of bread, but in exchange they wanted the money that their grandfather had given her for the alleged purchase of her brain. The old lady cupped her hand behind her ear: Huh? "The money!" yelled the Winterlings. She considered them with a smile. Then she recounted again what had happened the day Don Reinaldo passed by, staring at her fixedly and telling her that she had a brain like the Cathedral of Santiago. She told that story to everyone, because that day had been one of the happiest in her life.

The Winterlings responded that they'd heard this all before and that what they needed was the money.

The old lady sucked in her cheeks with a squelch.

141

"Girls, they were very bad to your grandfather," she said, as she turned her sausage on the fire.

They'd heard that, the Winterlings replied. But they didn't know why. Their memory of it wasn't quite right—they'd been little girls when everything happened—but what they wanted now was the money that was due to them as Don Reinaldo's granddaughters.

The old lady pulled her sausage off the stick. She cut off a chunk of bread and made herself a sandwich. She chewed with the few teeth she had and began to speak with a full mouth.

"Don Manuel, the priest, used to have plenty of these sausages in his basement. And he had salamis, olives, tinned sardines, haricot beans, preserves, packets of cookies . . . That chubby fellow had quite a stash! When they found him out, he was very nervous. It was for the whole town, he argued, he was just *administering* it . . . And he said his mother was very old and weak and needed to eat . . . But his mother was already dead by then, although no one found out for days afterward!"

The Winterlings said that they remembered how the priest's mother had been sick and didn't leave the house during the day.

"She didn't need to go out," answered the old lady immediately. "She already had her son to tell her everyone else's private business. Listen, once I went to confess a sin of lust, and the very next day, when I went past the priest's house, his mother hissed at me from the window and beckoned me inside. She told me that what I was doing was very bad and even gave me penitence. From that day on, I never confessed again to the priest . . . "

The old lady from Bocelo scratched her nearly hairless head with a bony finger.

"In any case, those doctors from Santiago, with their black suits as shiny as beetles, they ended up coming anyway when Old Lady

Resurrección kicked the bucket, even though her son tried to hide it. Just like when that maid Esperanza died . . . Anyway, I was telling you how they didn't believe him and were going to punish him, so Don Manuel bought them off by telling them about Don Reinaldo's business. It was him who told them that your grandfather used to gather a group of doctors, poets, and mayors around the hearth and such and, I don't know, that they had organized a committee for the redistribution of work, crops, and wealth."

She got up and lifted her mattress. A wad of cash appeared. Saladina gathered it up and quickly put it in her apron pocket. After a while, she pulled out a corner of the wad to inspect it on the sly.

"The money's yours, my girls, I feel better that way," said the old lady. "The priest already told me you handed back his contract and that he has it tucked away safely. You know the only regret I have? I wish I'd seen the Cathedral of Santiago. They say it's very pretty and many people go there to fulfill promises . . . Now, if you don't mind, let me rest a while. I've got so much sleep to catch up on . . . "

A few days later, the old lady died.

The priest had gone up to the hut in his usual weary, bad mood. He found the old lady sitting up. Waiting for him.

"Father," she said, with eyes as wide as dinner plates, "I know what's happened. God has forgotten about me."

"Come on, woman!"

"I'm a hundred and ten years old." She held up her hand and started counting her fingers. "You see, I've been counting. During the phylloxera plague of 1880, I was a young lady of about forty. Either God can't count or he's forgotten about me," she repeated, totally convinced.

143

The two of them went into the hut.

"Rest a while, woman, and I'll stay here and pray, reminding God just how old you are."

"You'll tell him I'm a hundred and ten? It's important to remind him of the exact number."

"I'll do it right now. You have a little rest and I'll make sure to tell him, given I've got a direct line."

The old lady got into bed and covered herself with a disgusting blanket.

"Tell him about the phylloxera plague, that ought to remind him." She was silent for a while, then her mouth started making noises. "You know what I'd like, Father?"

The priest shook his head.

"To see the Cathedral of Santiago. They say many people who have made promises go there."

"That's true," said the priest. "The pilgrims."

The old lady's eyes began to droop.

"Thank you for reminding our Lord about my age. It's only normal that he forgets the details, there are so many of us!"

Don Manuel began to pray.

"I'd also be thankful if when I died, you could take me down to your house for the wake. I'm scared that someone will do to me what they did to your mother!"

"Dear lady!"

But when Don Manuel went to say goodbye, see you tomorrow, like he did every day, the old lady had died.

The priest felt so moved (and he wasn't quite sure why, but so *guilty*) that he decided to fulfill the old lady's last wish and hold the wake in his own house. And so that nothing and no one was missing, he served a funeral banquet and had the maid prepare dried apricots. He even hired a *choradeira*, or professional mourner, who was a friend of Aunty Esteba.

As expected, everyone came to the wake. After they double-checked that the old lady was dead (there were still people who couldn't believe it) and had kept vigil over her for a while, they tucked into the bacon, the cakes, and the salami, and the local wine served in the next room, and got to telling each other tales about hidden treasures and folks who had come back from far-off lands transformed into chickens.

The Winterlings didn't miss it either. When it was time to go, Dolores wanted to say farewell to the old lady one last time.

She entered the room silently and, to her surprise, discovered that the old woman was not alone. There was Mr. Tenderlove, leaning over her. It looked like he was whispering something to her, or fixing up her collar, or maybe gently placing a necklace on her. She came up a bit closer, from behind. No, he wasn't talking to her. What did Mr. Tenderlove have in his hands? Pliers. Everything played out as if in a dream.

Dolores watched as the dental mechanic carefully extracted the three or four teeth that the poor old lady had left.

She ran out of there as quickly as she could.

5

CAMERAS, LIGHTS, false backdrops, fishermen working as extras, gypsies, a bullfighter, Americans in hats everywhere, the light and heat of the Mediterranean, the houses whitewashed and decorated with flowers . . . When those foreign men asked her to undress, she didn't get upset. In the end, that was what why she was there, and her sister had already warned her that she would have to do the nude scenes that nobody else wanted to do. It's not as if she enjoyed them seeing her like that, but she also knew that this was her big opportunity. She pulled down her skirt, took off her underwear, and unbuttoned her blouse.

Her breasts burst out, seeking the freedom they had been denied for so many years.

Cupping them delicately in the palms of his hands, one of the men measured and weighed her breasts, as if the whole business hung on their size and weight. Dolores closed her eyes. While one hand slid slowly over her arms and armpits, she felt the other one touch her belly button. And then another one on her pelvis. There was too much hand in that area. "Relax, Dolores," she told herself. "This will be over soon."

Dolores opened her eyes. A man with octopus eyes was watching her with a smile. There was laughter, or worse, ridicule, in that look. After a while, the man disappeared, leaving her alone in front of the cameras. But she realized with horror that he had penetrated her neckline and that a cold gelatinous mass was advancing over her breasts. "Relax, we'll be finished soon," she heard again. "It's lucky you got this role, considering how many women showed up for the screen tests. You'll be a part of cinema history." "Yes, I'm up for it," she replied. She had closed her eyes again when she heard the waterfall voice of her sister.

"Who are you talking to, Dolores?"

Dolores woke up. She was trembling, her nightdress was in a twist, and she was bathed in sweat. It was nothing more than a dream. But she had been left with a real feeling in her heart: inside the kingdom of remorse lived a slimy octopus.

A few days later, she was assaulted by the very same dream, and she wanted to recount it to her sister, to unburden herself. She called out to her from her bed again and again, but when she received no answer, she lit the lantern. Her sister's bed was empty.

Then she thought that perhaps she might be in the kitchen, absorbed in one of her lists or eating figs.

But she wasn't in the kitchen.

She wasn't in the orchard, the chicken yard, on the mountain, or in the river.

She wasn't at Mr. Tenderlove's office either; he explained to her that just the day before, he'd installed the final tooth.

Just when she was beginning to worry, Dolores found a note stuck to the Singer:

I'll be back soon, Dólor, don't worry about me.

Your beloved sister, Saladina.

She wasn't worried, but the next day Dolores felt profoundly alone. Alone and bewildered. Where could that silly girl have gone? At dawn, she sought comfort in her daily chores. She fed the chickens, milked Greta the cow, and took the animals out to graze. She would have to make curd cheese and some more fig jam for when her sister returned. It was Saladina's favorite dessert, although Dolores didn't want to show weakness by making a grand gesture. She gathered a great deal of kindling to fill the woodshed; Saladina was always complaining that there was no point in having one if it was always empty. One of the sheep was pregnant; Saladina would be excited to see that!

But the next day Saladina still wasn't there.

The third day was the hardest of all. The weight of loneliness was mixed with a sordid sense of relief. Wasn't this what she had always wanted? But Dolores could barely get out of bed. She had woken up with the terrible certainty that Saladina was lost somewhere. Finally, she got going. If her sister were to return at that very moment, she wouldn't like seeing her like that, sad and idle.

On the mountain, right in the middle of the day, she felt afraid. Later on, she searched for her with some of the villagers until it began to get dark.

Saladina didn't come back at nightfall either.

By the fourth day, she began to suspect that she might never see her sister again. But all her things were still there: her clothes, the bottle of anise. What would she do without the Singer? And it had cost her so much!

The hours became eternal. The house sank into silence. Without her sister there, feeling sorry for herself while she drank anise, complaining that Dolores was trying to kill her by putting stones in the lentils or treating her worse than the chickens, it was as if Dolores herself were not there. Just as she was about to go to bed, she heard the creaking of cartwheels and looked out the window. She let out a sigh of disappointment when she saw that it was Meis's Widow.

The Winterling opened the door. After eyeballing the whole house, examining the crumbling walls and rotten furniture hung with wet washing, and asking why she was all alone, the woman explained that she had come to reclaim the contract for the sale of her brain. Dolores said that she had no such thing, to which the Widow replied that she should save her stories, because before dying, the old woman from Bocelo had told everyone that she and her sister had kept the contracts and that half the village had theirs back already.

"It's not about us not being able to die without the contract, as the old lady thought," added the Widow. "It's that our lives stopped when we sold our brains, don't you understand? I need to tear up the piece of paper so I can start truly living again."

Then Meis's Widow told more stories. She went back in time, to the harsh January of 1936, when meat, coal, flour, and sugar began to be rationed in Tierra de Chá.

"We were all very hungry, and the only place we could find anything to eat was on the black market. But you needed money to pay for that. So then we found out that Don Reinaldo was paying handsomely just for signing a piece of paper. Nearly everyone in the village did it. We didn't realize what we had done until first Esperanza the maid died, and then Old Lady Resurrección, the priest's mother. You can't imagine the scandal that erupted in Tierra de Chá with those deaths. Doctors everywhere. And everything took place here"—she glanced around the house again—"in this house. Days and days locked up inside with the dead body . . ." Here the Widow paused. "You can't live if you've sold your brain . . ."

Dolores listened in astonishment.

"But Widow, you got married after the war, your life continued . . ."

Meis's Widow sighed. She took the Winterling by the arm and led her to the window. "Look over there," she said. "Can you see my house?"

In the distance, next to the church, she could see the chimney to the house where Uncle Rosendo and Meis's Widow lived. It was a humble home with a pitched roof, a pigeon loft, chickens in the yard . . .

"Do you know what lies beyond my house?"

Dolores said that she didn't know.

"There is a wall."

"A wall?"

"Yes, a wall. And do you know what lies beyond the wall?"

"No."

"*Absence*."

The Winterling felt a shiver.

"They say I got married . . . Yes . . . But . . . " The Widow trailed off and stood up. "If you don't want to give it to me, I'll find it myself!" she added.

Trailed by Dolores, she began to move furniture and open drawers in the kitchen. She went up to the bedroom, turned everything upside down, caught sight of the trapdoor, opened it, looked, saw the cow, and went down to the stable. She was already lifting up the bed of gorse when the Winterling grabbed her by the arm. She looked at her with such resolution that the Widow yielded.

She told her to stop looking and get out of there at once.

That night, Dolores searched for Saladina's smell on her pillow and cried for the first time since she had left.

At midday, on the way up the mountain, she came across the priest pulling his cart. He told her that he had been dining with the mayor of Sanclás, who had once again insisted that the sisters had to make a statement before a judge in Coruña. He said that if they didn't go, the Civil Guard would come to take them. Dolores promised that they would do it soon. (Stupid, foul-smelling priest. *Woolly bear caterpillar.*)

On her way back, three or four hours later, she stopped in front of Tristán's house. She was feeling scared and alone, she needed to talk to someone, and she remembered that, in fact, the rooster raiser still hadn't diagnosed the chickens' strange illness. And so she tied Greta to a tree and decided to go inside. She found him upstairs, asleep among his capons. On the bench in the living room, blackened from smoke and grease, crows, silky-smooth bats, and other birds of all sizes and colors had made their nests. From time to time, one of them got up and flew around in the room's strange blue air, almost as if it were the forest.

Dolores tapped on Tristán's arm a few times, and he woke up with a fright. He began to look around himself, muttering that he was in a hurry, that he had to arrive *well before* nightfall. A few seconds later, he realized he was in his own house, and he calmed down. Then Dolores explained to him that her chickens were still playing up. They spent the whole day scratching and fighting beneath the fig tree. *And when I . . .*

"Clearly, it's a case of jealousy," Tristán interrupted.

"Jealousy?" asked the Winterling, taken aback.

Tristán explained that all groups of chickens, just like all groups of humans, become accustomed to their own internal laws, their own way of life, and, above all, their own hierarchy. If a rooster comes into the group, he will naturally occupy the top spot, and the hens will have their place beneath him. No chicken wants to end up on the bottom, and so they defend themselves by pecking and engaging in savage fights. The bigger the group, the longer and more complicated the transition process will be.

Dolores listened to him, perplexed.

"And the poop?"

Tristán replied that it was important to get to the heart of the matter, which wasn't the poop but the chicken.

He got up, grabbed a ball of dough, pulled a nearby capon toward him, and stuffed the dough in its mouth.

"Listen, Winterling. I can't hold out any longer. I've got to ask you for my piece of paper as well . . . "

"Your piece of paper?" she asked, feigning ignorance.

"The contract of sale for my brain," he said. "I can't stand it anymore. These little monsters are driving me crazy. Tied up all day to this routine . . . *I'm not made for this*. I need to start living again!"

The capon was refusing to eat, and Tristán started on a string of insults. Dolores disappeared downstairs without another word.

When she arrived home, she decided to sew in order to stop thinking about her sister. But while she got her work out, she couldn't stop thinking about what the rooster raiser had told her. Jealousy? Hierarchy? Chickens don't have the brains to feel jealousy! And the piece of paper! Tristán wanted his contract, too! She was sick of this business about the brains!

Just as she was about to start the Singer, she heard something outside that sounded like footsteps on the staircase; she'd thought she had heard them the previous night as well, but they had been rats. "Good God, what's in store for us?" she exclaimed, and heard the creaking of the back door.

Saladina came inside like a nighttime fog, lean and haggard, with her brow furrowed and her face twisted into a grimace.

As soon as she had walked through the door, her sister sobbed and hugged her, telling her that they had combed the mountain looking for her, that both Meis's Widow and Tristán had demanded their contracts . . . Most of all, she wanted to know where she had been, what had been so important that she'd taken off like that without telling Dolores.

"I was worried sick about you. I love you very much, Saladina, and I don't care that you're seeing the dental mechanic. I'm not jealous. I'm not going to start pecking at you, but tell me where you were . . . "

"Shut your mouth!" replied her sister.

Dolores obeyed.

Saladina told her to stop the lecturing, that she wasn't a chicken, and that she, too, had her own private business, and to leave her alone, because she had a sore stomach.

"Were you eating figs out there?"

"No!"

From then on, there was no more discussion. Dolores turned on the Singer and began to sew. She'd barely had a wink of sleep in the four days her sister was missing, and now, happy and relaxed, she fell asleep hunched over the machine. She woke up feeling that a great deal of time had passed. She heard voices in the orchard.

"Get down, woman, don't be silly! You're too young for this."

"I'm killing myself! There's no other way!"

"Get down!"

"My guts hurt!"

She went to the window. At the very top of the fig tree, among ripe figs, astride a branch that was about to snap, Saladina sat perched like a big, ugly, disheveled bird.

From down below, a woman from the village was yelling up at her.

"What if you stopped talking to the sheep?"

There was another woman, who sounded like Meis's Widow.

"We all want to change, oh yes, to be different, how nice that would be. But think of your sister, all alone. Think about it for a second. Do you want her to die of sadness?"

Dolores heard a rustling in the branches. Then came Saladina's voice.

"I'm killing myself! There's no other way! Nobody loves me!"

Beneath the fig tree, next to the spot where the chickens scratched and fought, more and more people were gathering. Some of the women were crying, although, in the depths of those moist eyes, you could tell that they were enjoying themselves. Uncle Rosendo, who was also there, had a hint of song in his voice.

"You'll have plenty of time to kill yourself. Look, here comes your sister . . . "

When Dolores appeared, everybody went quiet. Then a voice like thunder shattered the silence.

"Sweet Mother of Jesus! And what the hell are you doing up there?" She waved her hands four or five times to get the chickens off her feet. "Missing for four days, and then as soon as you're back, you climb up the fig tree and say you're going to kill yourself?"

Silence. The chickens pecked at each other more than ever. Uncle Rosendo kicked at one, which flew off. After a while, Saladina's voice could be heard again.

"I'm killing myself, Dolores. I'm jumping. Nobody loves me. I'm miserable!"

"You're going to jump? After all that time I've spent looking after you?"

A fig fell off the tree, *splat*, and burst all over the ground like the insides of an animal. The bystanders, thinking that Saladina could end up like that, too, let out a gasp.

But Saladina was clinging to the branch and didn't fall.

"*You* looking after *me*? More like the other way around . . . Remember all that about your Tomás. If it weren't for me, you'd still be there, eating octopus with him in that horrible house. Don't you remember? All men are the same! All men are shameless! They're bastards!"

"You should remember, Sala, how lonely you were when I left."

"And you should remember, Dolores, how that bastard was going to kill you, but . . . "

"Shut up!" shouted Dolores from below.

"Yes, shut up!" answered Saladina from above. "Now I think we should both shut up."

"Put up and shut up!" they yelled in unison.

Just then, Don Manuel, the priest, showed up.

"My little sheep gone astray!" he yelled to Saladina. "But what is this that they're telling me you're going to do?"

Hearing the priest's voice, Saladina redoubled her efforts.

"I'm not coming down—no way! I'm going to jump! Anyway, my stomach hurts!"

Don Manuel pulled out a bottle from under the folds of his cloak.

"Come down for a drink, and you'll see how you're an entirely new person, my girl," he yelled.

But Saladina wouldn't see reason. Between sobs, she began to ramble on about how cruel men are and how undeserving they are of women's love. Because they always do the same thing, they wait for the woman to give in and then—ow, ow, my stomach hurts! On the count of ten, I'm jumping. And then she began to count: one, two . . .

Everyone on the ground joined in: three, four, five . . . The chickens scratched at the ground. Right at that moment, Mr. Tenderlove came running down the road.

"Sala!" he yelled from a distance. "Forgive me! I didn't mean to hurt your feelings!"

When she heard his voice, Saladina began to tremble nervously.

"What are you doing here, you little fairy? Where did you leave your wig, you fag, you hairy wart?" She yelled until the branch began to crack, and once again everyone down below gasped! They kept counting: six, seven . . .

"Fairy?" asked the priest.

"A bottle, you say?" answered Saladina.

"Of local wine," said Don Manuel.

"Eight, nine . . . " continued Saladina. Then, suddenly, she stopped. "Fine, I'm coming down," she said. "For a drink."

With great difficulty, Saladina managed to climb down the fig tree. But when she touched the ground, she doubled over in pain. Before the Winterlings could make it into the house, several of the women came up to Dolores and said that they wanted their contract of sale. Again? That's enough! Sick of it all, Dolores yelled that they didn't have the contracts and that they wouldn't speak of it again. Never again!

The women took a step back.

There was a general silence.

Dolores shooed off the chickens and took her sister inside the house.

6

ONCE SHE WAS INSIDE, Saladina, between mouthfuls of anise, told Dolores what had happened. Or rather, *some* of what had happened.

She had gone back to Tenderlove's office, because he had told her that at last he had the remaining teeth to complete her mouth. And so, during this final visit, the dental mechanic had finished the job. The new teeth had turned out spectacularly; there were three slightly yellow teeth, but what did that matter? Saladina was more beautiful than ever before. That's exactly what an exultant Tenderlove told her as she went up to the mirror to see.

"You're back to your old self," he told her. "I always had my eye on you, not your sister."

"I've got some money here to pay you, Tender," she said, without taking her eyes off the mirror, making a dreamy come-hither look in the style of a Hollywood actress. "How much do I owe you?"

"We'll talk about it later. That's not what interests me at the moment . . . "

That Tenderlove, Saladina thought to herself. *Always with his ambiguous answers . . .*

"Did you bring me what I asked for?" asked Tenderlove shyly.

Saladina began rummaging through her handbag.

"Now then . . . let's see . . . did I bring it?" she said, pretending to look.

Saladina was so nervous that she decided to ask for permission to use the bathroom, where she would be able to catch her breath and look at her new teeth in peace. The dental mechanic explained where it was, and she drifted out as if on a cloud, opening and closing her mouth like a piranha to make sure that the teeth matched up. In fact, they didn't match up at all. Suddenly, she found herself in a room that was totally different from all the others in the house.

No, it certainly wasn't the bathroom.

It was a room that stood in stark contrast to the simplicity of the office. It was ornately decorated with velvet curtains, pink walls, and a faint aroma of roses or jasmine—the same sweet fragrance that Tenderlove gave off some mornings. It was so intoxicating, especially when he leaned over her to work on her mouth. Everything in there was feminine; there was an open wardrobe hung with dresses of every color, length, and style. There were frou-frous, overblown wigs, necklaces. There were also high-heeled shoes. Saladina's heart skipped a beat. What was all this? Was Tenderlove married? Perhaps he had a lover? *No*, she told herself immediately. They would have said something in the tavern. That couldn't be it. They would've seen her around Tierra de Chá. She kept looking. By the window, there was a dressing table covered in bottles of perfume, lipsticks, powder compacts, and oils.

She got out of there as quickly as she could. In the office, she went to get her bag and leave. She was so distraught she didn't know where to look.

"Are you looking for something?" asked Tenderlove.

The night before, spread out on the bed under the sheets, Saladina had fantasized about that day's visit. Finally, she would have a whole set of teeth, and he would tell her how beautiful she looked. She would reply with some comment, something daring and rapturous, a little bit obscene perhaps, and then Tenderlove would come toward her.

Without the necessary period there ought to be between modesty and excessive familiarity, Tenderlove would tell her, "I want to see you naked." And because she wouldn't react and would instead stand there with her mouth agape, the dental mechanic would grab her firmly by the waist, pull her toward him, and tear at her skirts and undergarments. With one hand, he would reach for his scissors and cut away what he could of the underwear and brassiere, slip, blouse, pouch, pinafore, and cardigan, and tear off what remained with his teeth. A wild beast. Her stockings ripped. A clog flying through the air.

At last, when he had her in front of him, with her breasts standing erect and her thighs vibrating, he would let out an animal howl. That was when she would take the opportunity to throw him down on the table, sit on top of him, and beat down on his chest with her other clog, until *whoosh*, it would fly through the air and out the window.

She had envisaged all of this while lying down on the bed. Feverish, burning with desire. Her fantasy was so real that when she came out of it, it took a good while for her to figure out how she had gotten from the dental mechanic's house back to her own bedroom.

"My handbag," she said now with a mere shred of her voice. "I'm looking for my handbag . . . "

Her handbag had fallen behind the chest of drawers.

Saladina had just caught sight of it and was bending over to pick it up. He was standing behind her, and when she stood up they brushed cheeks.

Saladina was startled. What you experienced beneath your bedsheets was one thing, and harsh reality another. And in the harsh reality of life, everything to do with the world of men filled her with confusion: it was a wasteland of frost and wolves. She became confused if she saw a bull mount a cow in the countryside, and if sex ever came up in conversation, she would block her ears. The very word made her think of the damp in the attic.

But that wasn't sex, nor would it be. No. It was nothing—perhaps a gesture, an approximation, a butterfly, a movement in the air. It seemed so natural that, for the first time in her life, she wondered how she could have existed up to this point without ever having been touched by a man.

Suddenly, Tenderlove pushed her against the table and sought her lips. She steadied herself and brushed off the tool tray with her hand. The spatulas, calipers, and bones fell to the ground with a sound like broken glass. Was this happening under the covers? She didn't know. She turned her face away, she turned it into his.

It was the first time a man had kissed her, and, although she enjoyed the kiss—it was soft and wet, and had the sweet flavor of figs—she immediately confused it with sex.

A kiss was sex, and sex was a sin.

Sin was illness.

She grabbed her bag and prepared to leave. Before they separated, Tenderlove spoke.

"You went into the pink room, didn't you?"

Saladina nodded.

"It was my mother's room. It's exactly as it was before she died."

Saladina left the office flushed. Sex. Sin. Mother. Not only was he a cultured, attractive man, but also warm and shy and sentimental. How she adored men with a secret soft side! *His* mother, *and there was me thinking the pink room belonged to some woman.* A blur of feelings crowded her mind.

She was so happy, so sure of herself, that she decided that she would pursue the crazy idea that had been swirling around her mind ever since Dolores had told her about the Ava Gardner movie.

Now she could do it, too. What did her sister think? That she liked sewing ball dresses for little rich girls?

Once she got home, she put the bare minimum in a suitcase and took the money the old lady from the mountain had given them and Tenderlove didn't seem to want. She took a bus to Coruña, and from there, a train to Madrid. Nearly a day later, she arrived at Tossa de Mar with the intention of being chosen as Ava Gardner's body double.

But she didn't reveal this part to Dolores. Instead she told her that she had gone to Coruña to speak with the judge and, despite much searching, was unable to find him.

The pretty one and the ugly one. She still recalled that incursion into the world of cinema with bittersweet emotion. Many afternoons, sitting in front of the Singer, images of the filming swirled around in her head. How beautiful it had all been in the beginning! The two sisters strolled through the streets of a small English town while the camera followed them. Everyone fussing over them. They met up with people, picked flowers, bought bread . . . The dialogue was confusing: it was in English, and the sisters never quite understood the script. But everything took place so naturally that nothing seemed out of place to them. Then one day, during a break, while they were being made up for the next scene, someone asked Saladina if she was the pretty one or the ugly one. She was arrayed in a fitted dress with nylon pleats, with several strings of false pearls and matching earrings, and plenty of rouge on her cheeks. "The ugly one?" asked Saladina, puzzled, adjusting her pearl necklace. "Yes," the other person said, "*the ugly one.*"

"Because you certainly aren't the pretty one . . . "

7

BUT THE TRIP to Tossa de Mar had been a failure. After waiting for a whole day in the bay, where *Pandora and the Flying Dutchman* was being filmed, lined up with the other women who had come to the casting call for body doubles, dying from the heat and loneliness, they didn't even give her the chance to display her acting skills.

Perhaps it was the last opportunity she could find in her wounded heart, or perhaps she was guided by the same ancestral instinct she had felt the last time she was there, but without knowing why, Saladina returned to Tenderlove's office as soon as she arrived back in Tierra de Chá. She had no reason to go there; her teeth were complete. Seeing her come in, Tenderlove felt his knees going weak. He knew straight away that she wasn't there on a professional visit.

"Sit down in the chair and I'll take a look," he said nonetheless.

Saladina was feeling docile and dazed. She sat down, her legs firmly crossed. The skin on her face was sallow, full of fine cracks, like a crumpled-up piece of paper. From the dust on her clothes and the tired look on her face, you could tell she had been halfway around the world, but Tenderlove didn't want to ask any questions. She opened her mouth the way she did every time she sat down there. As the dentist leaned over her, she could smell the haze of jasmine around him. Or was it lilies?

Tenderlove, too, could smell the stench coming from Saladina's mouth: garlic and onions.

"No," said Tenderlove, jerking his head away. "Better not. Phwoah, what have you been eating? Close your mouth!"

She closed her mouth and awaited her second kiss, but Tenderlove disappeared. From somewhere she heard him speak: "I'm coming back now, don't open your eyes until I say. You have to know the truth."

After a while, when she was beginning to grow impatient, she heard his voice again: "You can open them now."

And so Saladina opened her eyes slowly. Before her stood a smiling Mr. Tenderlove, dressed as a woman.

He was wearing a flowered dress, high heels, and stockings (his hairy legs underneath). He had made up his face and put on a wig. He was smiling timidly.

"You've dressed up again, you rascal. Let's see if I can guess . . ."

But very seriously Tenderlove explained that this wasn't a costume. He said that this was who he was and that before things got more serious, he wanted her to know, because he had grown very fond of her. Sometimes, not always, but more and more often, he felt like a woman. "Now you know why I never quite fit in with them . . . the resistance fighters."

Saladina listened without blinking. Her blood tingled in her legs and stomach. Finally, she began to mumble.

"But you're dressed up . . . you . . . you like to play at . . . you kissed me."

Tenderlove explained again that this wasn't a costume and that sometimes, not always, but more and more often, he felt like a woman.

Saladina's chin began to tremble.

"You fairy!" was the only thing she could manage to say.

That was when she returned home. After drily greeting her sister, she spent quite a while without moving, her arms hanging down by her sides, her chin on her chest. She was thinking, what was she thinking?

Shortly after, she climbed up the fig tree.

8

ALTHOUGH SHE HAD BEEN very confused and worried during the four days that Saladina was missing, especially when they were combing the mountain for her, Dolores also made the most of that time to gather information about the dark acts that took place during the war.

Every time they spoke to her about "what happened back then," there was such an air of distrust that someone ended up recommending (almost demanding) that it was best not to talk about it.

"It" meant "when your grandfather was alive." Things had happened in the past that no longer took place, no longer existed, and of which nobody wished to speak. But one day, Tristán was in the tavern, and he started running his mouth. Someone called him a "greedy hermit, grumpy and strange like his capons," to which he replied that it was thanks to him and his capons that they'd all survived when Don Reinaldo had imposed the rationing of goods.

As soon as the war started, oil, sugar, and tobacco became scarce in Tierra de Chá, and that's when Don Reinaldo began to get everyone organized. Taking advantage of the cover of night, he distributed the goods (he mostly took them away from the priest and gave them to the others) and organized the division of farm work. Even Don Manuel was forced to grow potatoes, with his cassock tied up around his waist. One night, a pair of Civil Guards came to the house, broke up the meeting, and took Don Reinaldo to spend a night in prison.

Upon his return, the priest spoke with him. He told him that all this equal redistribution was going to cause them a lot of problems.

"But why?" Don Reinaldo wanted to know. "Didn't Christ preach something similar? If we don't share what we have, then it'll just belong to a handful of landowners and, in the end, to you."

Don Manuel reminded him that they'd done something similar in a nearby town and the government had forced them to hand over everything they owned.

"Don't you understand?" added the priest. "We'll be left with nothing, and what's more, we'll draw attention to ourselves."

"There are already plenty of people who have nothing."

But Don Manuel, fearful of going hungry, kept grumbling.

"Don't be so stubborn, Reinaldo."

In the village, there were more and more checkpoints and searches. The villagers still took their animals to graze on the mountain, but now there were guards patrolling the meadows with orders to shoot on sight. At dusk, a truck arrived and two men jumped down with pistols tucked into their belts. "Long live Spain!" they yelled out, and everyone rushed out into the plaza, their arms out straight in salute and repeated "Long live Spain!"

One night, a poet-friend of Don Reinaldo's arrived by the hearth. He said that in Coruña, the military had overthrown the civil government. Meis's Widow, Gumersinda with her limp, Aunty Esteba, and Esperanza the maid all burst into tears.

People said that ever since the king had fled, the world had stopped turning.

They began to take people away in trucks, corpses appeared in ditches, and there were checkpoints on every road. One day, Don Reinaldo, who was on his way to attend to a sick woman, came across Tenderlove beside the road. "What are you doing?" he asked, seeing him down in a ditch. "You're not 'prospecting' again, are you?" Tenderlove answered him by saying, "It's a donkey." "Donkeys don't have gold teeth," Don Reinaldo replied.

They'd already taken Don Reinaldo away once, and rumor had it that if they came back for him again, he'd never return. That was when he told his granddaughters to run away, far, as far as possible, and not to come back for as long as they could. He prepared some packs for them and left them in the forest. But a few days later, the girls had already returned.

The people in the village were restless. It was rumored that Uncle Rosendo was going to be taken away as well, for reciting poems that conflicted with sacred Catholic values. Don Manuel spoke again with Don Reinaldo. The priest was hungry, and had even lost weight. It just wasn't possible for all that food to be requisitioned. If he didn't eat, he couldn't give Mass. "So don't give it," replied Don Reinaldo. "You can see how little good it does in times like these." A silent hatred grew between them.

Then, at dawn one day, they came back for Don Reinaldo. They came looking for him, and when they couldn't find him, their first response was to beat the hell out of Uncle Rosendo. The military had occupied the square, and it was rumored that they'd killed some of the poor folks in nearby Bocelo. The whole village was terrified, and nobody wanted to leave their homes. Near the main road, under some scrub, the abandoned bodies of a poet and a left-wing councilman appeared. Someone had pulled out their teeth.

Don Reinaldo spent nearly the whole day in hiding. Only Don Manuel, the priest, knew where he was.

The whole village felt threatened, although nothing had happened yet. One day, Mr. Tenderlove went to see the priest. He asked him if he was hungry.

"Well, of course!" said the priest, relieved that someone else was also thinking about food. "I can barely think. My guts are rumbling and my legs are wobbly." He looked at Tenderlove out of the corner of his eye. "And yourself? Aren't you hungry?"

"Very," he replied.

Then Don Manuel said that there was a solution. "In his stockpile, Don Reinaldo has tins of sardines, pasta, bacon, chorizo . . . who knows what else! It's time to get it all out and share it out now. The war won't last long."

Tenderlove agreed and said he would be telling Don Reinaldo. He'd try to reason with him. But there was one problem: only the priest knew where he was hiding.

9

ONE MORNING, shortly after the episode of her sister's flight and dramatic return, Dolores got up with the feeling that before things got any worse, she had to go to Coruña to tell a few lies to that judge who was trying to track them down.

So she put a few things in a bag and went down to the square to wait for the bus. Two hours later, she was in Coruña.

It was difficult to find the person who was looking for them, mostly because she didn't know—*or wasn't sure she knew*—why he was looking for them in the first place. But after going around and around through the corridors of the courts, they finally told her that there was only one judge for the county she lived in and that he was just over there, working in his office.

The interview lasted a little more than twenty minutes. When she went back out into the street, Dolores adjusted her skirt and sighed with relief. The judge hadn't wished to interrogate her about Tomás, her Tomás, but about Ramón, the maid's son. After all, he had died in their stable, and the judge was obliged to determine the circumstances of his death.

On the way to the station, where she intended to take the bus home, she once again felt a cold shiver climb up her spine. An idea was forming in her mind, but she couldn't think very clearly. A few days before, she had come across Uncle Rosendo in the fields. They talked about the weather, the chickens, and the harvest, and then the country teacher asked her about that idea she had had about auditioning to be a double in that American movie. "The Ava Gardner movie?" asked the Winterling. "That's the one," said Uncle Rosendo, and with great assurance he added, "Don't forget to go."

There, in the middle of the fields, beneath the clouds and the sun of Tierra de Chá, next to the unmoving cows that grazed in the meadow, the country teacher told her about the moment of truth in everybody's lives. "That's yours," he said. "And because you're not there auditioning as a double, you'll never again have the opportunity to be an actress." That Ava girl didn't come to Spain to get away from Frank Sinatra. Oh no. She didn't even come to make a movie. Nothing ever just happens, and Ava Gardner had come to Spain exclusively so that she, Dolores the Winterling, could have the opportunity to meet her and become an actress. That's how the moment of truth works.

"Yes . . . " Dolores said thoughtfully. "It was only a coincidence that I was feeding the chickens at the time I heard the news . . . "

Uncle Rosendo said that coincidence does not exist.

Then Dolores told him that this kind of talk scared her. Uncle Rosendo replied that just like there's no smoke without fire, fear was the hint of a hidden emotion. He said that fear, like failure, formed part of the mechanics of the moment of truth. That's exactly what he said: "mechanics of the moment," as if he were speaking about the cogs of a watch.

Then he told her something that he had never revealed to anyone about that day he had gone to Coruña to requalify as a country teacher. He told her that at the moment when the tribunal asked his name, at that exact moment, something terrible had happened: he wet himself.

"Yes, you heard right—I wet myself. They said 'name' and I said 'Rosendo.' And I can't remember a thing after that. I wanted to say

my surname, but I couldn't get it out. I couldn't remember my surname, or where I came from, or even how old I was or how long I'd
been teaching. My vision went blurry, and then I felt the warmth.
And then the wetness. And even so, I passed."

At the ticket counter, just as she was about to buy her ticket home,
Dolores smiled and remembered the story. What if Uncle Rosendo's
theory was true? She let the people behind her pass and sat down on
a bench. She put her bag down on the ground. Without realizing,
she began squeezing her breasts through her blouse. She'd seen how
the judge was staring at them. She got back in the line for the ticket
counter, feeling the beginnings of a powerful force growing inside
her. Then, instead of saying "one ticket to Tierra de Chá" she came
out with "one ticket to Girona."

Three or four days later, back in Tierra de Chá, as she came down
the path, she saw that her sister had been pruning the fig tree. The
chickens were still scratching in the same spot (there they all were,
stupid and insistent) as if there were no more to the orchard than
that tiny patch of dirt, as if that tiny patch of dirt covered in poop,
feed, and stale bread was the entire world. She found her sister in
the kitchen, her head down, her nose running, and her face as dark
as a storm cloud.

"I know where you went," she heard as soon as she opened the
door.

As she went inside, Dolores looked around at the house. The
chairs were turned over, and the table was covered in dirty dishes,
seeds, and juice. Squashed figs littered the unswept floor, and
the shutters were half-open. As far as she could tell, Saladina
hadn't done a thing besides cry and eat figs the whole time she had
been away.

"They chose me," said Dolores with a smile, collapsing into a chair. "And they paid me. Heaps of money, Sala. We can do whatever we want with it. We won't have to sew anymore."

Saladina raised her head slowly. A flash of blood flicked across her eyes.

"They chose you?" she croaked.

Dolores smiled timidly.

"I'm an actress. Albert, you know . . . he's promised to give me more roles. He's already thinking about his next movie and . . . "

"Albert?"

"Albert Lewin. The director of *Pandora*. He's also the director of *The Picture of Dorian Gray*—you remember that movie where a man sells his soul to the devil in exchange for eternal youth? We saw it in Coruña. It turns out that the painting gets older but he doesn't . . . " Dolores paused, looked her sister over, and then kept talking. "Lewin is a producer for Metro-Goldwyn-Mayer."

"Sure he is . . . "

"In about two months, he's going to write to me with a firm offer for a romance in Technicolor! And listen . . . I've been dreaming of this moment for years. This time I'm not going to let the opportunity pass me by."

"For the love of God!" screeched her sister, clutching her stomach. "So . . . did you do the nude scene, when Pandora comes out of the sea in moonlight covered only in a ship's sail?"

Puzzled, Dolores said yes, that she had done the nude scene, that everyone had agreed that she had an amazing body, with curves, even better than Ava Gardner's some of them said, and . . . "But how did you know there was a nude scene? Only those who auditioned as extras know about that scene!"

Her sister writhed in pain.

"My stomach's a mess," was her response.

Dolores stood up.

"Answer me! How do you know about the nude scene? How? How do you know?"

Saladina stood up as well. She stumbled over to the couch and collapsed on it.

"The rooster raiser came for his contract, too!"

She went silent for a moment, then her guts let out a sad squelch.

"My stomach hurts, Dolores."

Dolores hurried over to help her. She stood there thinking for a while.

"Again with your stomach? Did you eat too many figs?"

"I swear I didn't! I haven't eaten figs for ages!"

"Could it have to do with your new mouth?" said Dolores. "The mouth and the stomach are one and the same."

"That's not it," sobbed Saladina. She was silent for a while. "You don't love me like you used to, Dolores."

"Don't start with that old story now," she said, staring at her.

"You don't love me like you used to, Dolores. You go and you leave me here alone, you put stones in my lentils, you don't love me . . . "

The next day, Saladina wasn't better but a lot worse. Dolores went to speak with Mr. Tenderlove, who told her that her sister had been complaining about her stomach for a while now. He assured her that these pains couldn't have anything to do with her new dentures and recommended that they see a doctor. There was no doctor in Tierra de Chá, so the Winterling had to call one from a nearby town, who promised to come by as soon as possible.

The next morning, when Dolores went out of the house to feed the chickens, she found Violeta da Cuqueira sitting on the bench near the doorway.

A shiver ran up her spine.

"What are you doing here?" she asked sharply.

Dolores knew that not long ago, Old Lady Violeta had foretold that three men from Sanclás would die, and they had. She had dreamed of three chestnuts falling, and when she woke up, she understood.

"Your sister's spirit came to me, I've come to warn you," Violeta replied, unperturbed.

Dolores told her that she wasn't in the mood to listen to fairy tales and that Violeta should go away.

"But when did you say her spirit appeared?" she added.

"Two days ago. Tonight she will die."

Dolores grabbed the broom and threatened to kill the old lady if she didn't leave.

"Who were you talking to?" asked her sister when she came upstairs. "I thought I heard voices."

"It was just the wind, woman. It's starting to blow from the north. See how it shakes the corn."

"Ah yes, the wind . . . Hey, does something smell rotten to you?"

Dolores sniffed at the air.

"Something stinks."

"Get me a clean nightshirt from the drawer," replied Saladina.

That same night, a fierce wind broke one of the windows and got into the sisters' bedroom.

10

OLD. TALL. DRY.

Saladina felt it arrive, with its violent stench of rotten apple. She felt it arrive and crawl over her sister's flesh as she slept by her side. *It's just the wind, woman, blowing in from the north.* She felt it arrive, dense and insistent. *Who were you talking to?* She felt it arrive, accompanied by its hushed music.

Death came down for the Winterling, reeking of decay. For a whole night, death fed on life. Death was not beautiful; it was just Saladina spread out on the bed in her clean nightdress. Death arrived, prowling like an animal with centuries-old hunger, secrets of blood, secrets of voices and flesh, barely whispering: "Come, Saladina, it's me, the only one everyone shall know. Don't you tremble at the sight of me? Take your suitcase of memories; take as many of them as you can, because you will go stripped of everything else. Come with me, I am here for you. Come on, Sala."

Saladina.

Hearing a thrashing in the sheets, Dolores lit the lantern. She was relieved to see her sister awake and pensive. Lucid, with her eyes open as wide as a fish, she stared at the wall.

"We should paint the roof," she heard her say.

"Yes," replied her sister, with a sigh of relief.

Saladina, who by now had sat up on the bed, cast an imposing figure. A thick branch of black hair hung down her back, all the way to her waist. The light of the lantern barely lit up her face, bringing out her harsh features—reminders of smallpox, scars and lines around the eyes—and giving her a strange, almost savage sense of beauty.

"The house is falling down around us."

"Yes . . . "

"Did you call the doctor?"

"Of course! He won't take long to come, you'll see."

"I'm not ready to kick the bucket yet."

"You won't kick anything."

"Dolores . . . "

Saladina was still rigid, sitting up in bed and staring straight ahead.

"What, Sala—what?"

"Don't go away again without me."

"No."

But Saladina was already crawling over to her sister's bed, making her way toward her thighs, kissing her navel and breasts, her armpit salty like the sea.

"The house is falling down around us."

" . . . "

Days later, the doctor from Sanclás appeared. That morning, Saladina was awake. Seeing him walk through the door, she began to tremble like a rabbit. The doctor asked Dolores how long she'd been like that, and Dolores said that she'd been complaining about her stomach for some time now. She also commented that she thought it might be due to the figs.

"How are you feeling?" asked the doctor, addressing Saladina.

Saladina twisted the sheets between her sweaty hands.

"You tell me! That's what doctors are for, aren't they?"

The doctor closed his eyes for a few seconds, as if stopping himself from taking the bait.

"I'll put it another way. What symptoms have you noticed?"

"Pain," she said. "It's because my guts are loose."

"Quite," replied the doctor.

"Sometimes some of them travel up to my gullet, and I can barely breathe," added Saladina, feeling very important with all this attention.

"Some of what?"

"My guts," she clarified. "And they cause little choking fits."

The doctor looked for his stethoscope in his doctor's bag.

"Can I ask you something, doctor?" asked Saladina while he listened to her breathing.

"Ask away . . ."

"What's happening to me now . . ."—she fixed her feverish pupils on his—"could it have anything to do with a kiss?"

"With a what?"

"With a kiss."

"Your abdominal pain?"

Saladina had the expectant look of someone waiting for an answer. She clicked her tongue like she used to when she had false teeth.

"No. Abdominal pain has nothing to do with kissing."

Saladina let out a large sigh.

"And is it contagious?"

"No, it's not contagious."

Saladina let out another sigh.

The doctor asked her more questions. Before he left, he spoke with Dolores in the doorway. Saladina would live a while longer, but she wouldn't get better. Stomach cancer was one of the worst illnesses. There was no treatment for it.

When the doctor left, Dolores went back up to the bedroom. She found Saladina looking much more calm.

"What else did the doctor tell you, Dolores?"

Dolores's legs were shaking. She could barely think.

"Nothing else. Just that you'll get better soon. You just need a bit more bed rest."

"More bed rest? My ass will get big."

A wave of sadness rolled over Dolores's eyes.

"You've got a lovely ass."

Shortly after, while Saladina was taking her siesta, Mr. Tenderlove knocked at the door. He said that the doctor from Sanclás had gone by his house to have a molar looked at and told him the news about Saladina.

"I'm truly sorry," he added.

"Sure . . . " said Dolores, not wanting to open the door fully.

The pair of them stood in silence.

"You two should never have come back," he said suddenly.

"But we did," she said, surprised by his comment. "We can't turn back time now."

"There is . . . There is a way," said Tenderlove.

Dolores opened the door a little more.

"All the village wants is to forget," he continued. "I know that your grandfather kept those contracts. If you hand them over to me, this will be over once and for all."

Dolores thought it over. Then she summoned the courage to do what she'd been thinking they ought to do for a while now. She set out for the orchard, followed by Mr. Tenderlove. She brushed off the chickens scratching around and crouched down under the fig tree. With her hands, she dug up a wooden chest that she handed over to the dental mechanic.

"Is your fire lit?" he asked, looking fixedly at the chest as he took it in his shaking hands.

The fire was lit, and they went back into the house. In front of the hearth, Tenderlove opened the chest with solemnity. The metal hinges were rusted over, but at last they were able to pull out a wad of tied-up envelopes that gave off a strong stench of earth and mold. One by one, with a look of disdain, he pulled them out and threw them in the fire. In barely a second, the envelopes opened up like the petals of a flower, then twisted and danced in the air before turning to tiny pieces. They began to fade and settle when through the open door a gust of wind blew in. The shreds of paper burned in the fire went up the chimney and into the sky. Tenderlove and the Winterling went out into the orchard. Now, the bits of paper floated down to the ground only to fly back up again, fluttering like tiny gray butterflies and settling on the trees, the fence posts, the pile of dry gorse in the square, and the tiled roofs of the houses of Tierra de Chá.

"It's raining," said Uncle Rosendo to his wife, looking at the sky from the other end of town, when they both went outside to look.

"Look, you dummy," the Widow replied, astonished by the spectacle of the little gray papers, resting her hand instinctively on her belly. "Can't you see they're butterflies?"

Rosendo squinted and looked again.

"They're moths," he said.

IT WAS A VAGUE MEMORY, melding in with the faces, gestures, and words of other men. Memory, always so wise, had silenced almost everything. Nevertheless, without realizing it, the people of Tierra de Chá had resolved many of their doubts about the grandfather.

A tall, strong, decisive man. A man with brilliant, nervous eyes the color of the sea. A man with a thin and scratchy yellow beard. A man in corduroy pants and jacket, sometimes a black tie. His pants were a brownish gray, old, the corduroy worn away from the wiping of hands, with patches over the knees. His jacket had elbow patches and was too big for him. A handsome man, and pleasing to the eye with his weather-beaten skin.

A good man (was he really good?) who was both a Christian and a communist. Interested in the sciences. At times, it had been said, a man of darkness. And stubborn. Something unknown moved inside him, like little roots entangled beneath the ground that have never seen the light of day, whose blind strength is the support for a beautiful plant of yellow flowers.

Don Reinaldo was the root of the gorse bush.

Gorse can be devastated by fire, pulled out by men, trampled by tractors, and yet it always sprouts again somewhere, time and time again, clinging onto the hillside or surviving next to the asphalt of the highway. That's how he was: a blind force out of which sprouted his wild delirium, his obsessions and eccentricities, and his youthful nostalgia. He had started studying medicine but never finished.

There was his obstinate desire to control and manage everyone around him, to make decisions for everybody else, to know more and more. The mad business of buying brains was what truly led him to his death.

Not long after Esperanza a la Puerta de Nicolasa died, there was cause for commotion in the village. The priest wanted to bury her immediately, but Don Reinaldo was set on keeping the body unburied for a few days. Cars carrying people in suits began to arrive in Tierra de Chá, mostly doctors from the Faculty of Medicine in Santiago. The Winterlings' grandfather put them up in his house, where they spent their days cooped up drinking cognac and doing who knows what.

A few of the villagers—the priest, Uncle Rosendo, and perhaps Tenderlove—confronted Don Reinaldo and demanded that the poor maid be buried. That was when he pulled out the contract for the sale of the brain, signed by the maid herself.

Don Manuel told Dolores all of this one morning. In fact, the Winterling had gone to him to get some weight off her own chest. She couldn't stop thinking about what had led them to seek refuge in this remote village and Mr. Tenderlove's comment that they should never have returned . . . In the beginning, Saladina had always spoken as if she, too, were involved in the whole business. But lately, it seemed she wanted to distance herself from it. Dolores noticed that her words had become more and more scathing.

And now she was convinced that her sister's illness had burst into their lives because of all this. And so, one September morning, with birds flitting about her and awash with strange aromas, she went to the priest's house. She found him eating breakfast by the stove. She said that she had come to confess but that there was no need to go to the church.

She told him that she couldn't stand it anymore, that she had a secret that wasn't just any old secret. It was about something dark and terrible, a secret she had wanted to reveal ever since they arrived in Tierra de Chá, but never had the courage to. It was about something that oppressed her, as if she were wearing a corset. It was something she had to tell, she had to do it, although she knew that once she did tell it, things would never be the same because—

"But what is it?" shouted the priest, throwing down his fork and waving his hands in the air.

So then Dolores confessed that she had been married to a certain Tomás, a fisherman of octopus and pout whiting from Santa Eugenia de Ribeira, just to escape the drudgery of routine and for the dream of leading a different life. But very soon, she discovered not only that she was not in love but also that her life was even more boring with him, she . . .

"I can't, Father. I can't tell you anymore . . . "

Don Manuel moved his dish of fried eggs and chorizo to one side. Lately, he had no appetite, and having no appetite bored him immensely. He was about to start speaking again when, without knowing why, he caught himself thinking that that was exactly what he used to say to his own mother: "I can't, I can't tell you anymore, Mother . . . " when she would ask him to tell her the secrets of all the people in the village.

He realized then that just before he began eating his fried eggs, he had been thinking of his mother—of her reddened hand after she slammed it down on the wooden table in the kitchen that day a long time ago, and of the sound it made, and of her words: "You will become a priest, and that's the end of it! So it's not a good idea for you to go around with women, women are bad, Manoliño . . . "

"Have you come to confess that you abandoned your poor husband?" he asked.

"No," answered the Winterling.

He wanted to keep asking, but he knew that he couldn't be too direct.

"And . . . this Tomás . . . if he is your husband, and you didn't abandon him, how is it that he is not here, with you?"

The Winterling told him that she couldn't tell him anything more, but that he shouldn't worry about the octopus fisherman, because he was quite at peace now. At peace forever.

The priest gulped.

12

DESPITE ALL THE BED REST recommended by the doctor, Saladina was feeling weaker and weaker. Each step was an effort. She sat down at the kitchen table with an appetite, but soon her stomach turned. She barely ate, and the pain was so bad that she couldn't sleep. Each morning, she got up feeling like her guts were loose, as she used to say. Dolores was completely devoted to her. Her life now took place next to her sister.

She didn't go up the mountain, she barely sewed, and she didn't even drop by the tavern.

She spent the whole day attending to Saladina, getting her to eat something and trying to relieve her pain; she was constant in her dedication and patience.

The illness had managed to sweeten Saladina's character and make her serene. But strangely enough, this serenity was exactly what puzzled Dolores the most. This apathetic woman was not her sister. Her surly temperament, her fervor, her unpleasantness was what made Saladina who she was. The resignation with which she now arose every morning to be cared for worried Dolores, and even made her suspicious. Saladina had always been impetuous and ill-tempered; she had always been the one to make decisions for both of them, but now she was just a rag doll. *It seems like she's just waiting for her time to come*, thought Dolores.

But one Monday in October, things seemed to take a turn. Just like every morning since she had returned from Tossa de Mar, Dolores went out to the orchard to see if the letter from Albert Lewin offering her a role in his next film had arrived.

"Where are you going?" asked Saladina.

"To find my destiny within the four walls of the letterbox," Dolores replied with irony.

But as always, there was nothing in the mailbox except cobwebs. Then she went to tend to Greta the cow, who was also growing weaker and weaker. When she was in the stable, she thought she heard a noise, and looked out the window.

Wrapped in a black cape, her arms in the air, Violeta da Cuqueira advanced slowly toward the house. When she arrived, she explained that someone from the village, whose name she couldn't reveal, had paid her to cure Saladina. Dolores got out the broom with the intention of beating her, but her sister, who had listened to the conversation from her bed, asked the witch to come up.

With the distant serenity that characterized her, the old woman took two bowls from a burlap sack and explained that she had come to wash her down with rye bran and give her a rub of pig fat. Hearing this, Saladina summoned the last of her strength and kicked off her covers and pulled up her nightdress, leaving her stomach exposed.

"I'm all yours, da Cuqueira," she said.

The next morning, after she'd been scrubbed three times with rye bran and rubbed down five times with pig fat, Saladina woke up clicking her tongue like in the old days.

She sat up on the bed, felt her stomach, and said that she felt like eating chorizo. Her sister advised against it and brought a simple broth instead. She didn't have the strength to get up, but they spent that day chatting, remembering old times, just like they used to when everything was fine. Saladina asked her sister to tell her a story. "A story" was always the same story: *Once upon a time there was a man called the Taragoña Express, who was all skin and bone, with a long scraggly beard . . .*

"Like Jesus Christ," clarified Saladina.

"Like Jesus Christ," continued Dolores, "who ran over twenty-five miles a day, and when he ran through the villages the people would come out to greet him and—"

"You forgot to say that he wore a loincloth."

"Well yes, that's right . . . He only wore a loincloth, and then one day—"

"You also forgot to tell how he ran through the cornfields . . . "

"Yes, through the cornfields and the tracks and the roads and the paths he would go, in the snow and the hail and the thunder and the pouring rain, in the scorching heat or in a storm until one day—"

"No one has come by for a while," Saladina cut in suddenly.

Dolores looked at her, puzzled.

"What do you mean?" she said.

"To ask for their piece of paper, the contract for the brain . . . "

Dolores went silent.

"Do you think they found them?"

Dolores the Winterling shrugged her shoulders.

At lunchtime, Saladina ate again with gusto. "Too much gusto," Dolores said to herself as she took the tray back to the kitchen.

That same afternoon, when Dolores bent down to tuck in her sister, Saladina pulled out her long, bony arms and wrapped them around her sister's neck. She gave her a kiss and, looking over her shoulder toward the sky, asked if it was night yet.

"No, why do you ask?" said her sister.

They stayed like that, watching the horizon, spellbound.

The sky was darkened by thousands of birds of all sizes and colors: owls, chickens, and capons. Hooting and clucking, they beat their wings slowly, flying blindly with their necks stretched out. Guided by an ancestral and powerful feeling, the Winterlings' chickens took flight as well, first clumsily and close to the ground, then calmly as they soared up to join the mass of birds that now floated over Bocelo Mountain, motionless.

Farther and farther away.

The next day, Saladina got up and swathed herself in blankets. She said that if the rubs had worked for her, they couldn't do any harm to the cow. She went down to the stable with the rye bran and the pig fat and spent a good while rubbing Greta Garbo's shrunken stomach, the poor cow not having the strength to protest. Exhausted by the effort, she sat down afterward by the hearth.

Dolores, happy to see her on her feet, lit the fire and prepared her breakfast. Then Saladina asked her to tell her in detail how it had all gone in Tossa de Mar.

"You really want to hear about that?" asked Dolores. "Maybe . . . maybe it's not the right time."

"Tell me!" demanded Saladina.

Swallowing bitter saliva, her face calm and exhausted, Saladina heard about all that Dolores had seen: the sea, the cameras, the lights, the costumes, the sets, the men. In the bay of Tossa, there was a headland on the beach itself, on which there was a little medieval citadel with seven circular towers. That's where they were filming. The shooting of *Pandora and the Flying Dutchman* began at seven in the morning and didn't finish until eight in the evening. The brightness was overwhelming, and for that reason, they had to put up black netting everywhere. They had been searching for doubles for more than two weeks, and despite all the women they had seen and interviewed, they still hadn't found anyone capable of doubling for the famous actress.

Just like every other day, the day Dolores arrived there was a long line of women waiting for a screen test. The Winterling asked where the end of the line was and waited her turn.

In the beginning, when they saw her dressed in her skirt, cable-knit cardigan, and provincial shawl, they didn't even think she had come to give a screen test. Then, when she let down her hair and told them in nearly perfect English that she had come to take the role of Ava's double in *Pandora and the Flying Dutchman*, that she had some but not much experience, and that she wouldn't do any nude scenes, they began to look at her more closely.

They were fascinated.

Albert Lewin told her about his new film and his intention to give her a contract.

"For a new movie? You, in the lead role?"

"Yes, in the lead role, I told you that when I got back, don't you remember?"

But for the moment, none of that was important. The important thing was for Saladina to get better, and until that happened, she wasn't going anywhere. The two of them would get out of the village as soon as they could, that was for sure.

"Does your stomach hurt, Sala?"

"No, it doesn't, Dolores. Since old Violeta came with her ointments, I feel much better."

Neither of them knew that at that moment, the illness was preparing to redouble its attack with brutal and unexpected force.

13

AROUND THAT TIME, the village was undergoing changes as well. The mayor of Sanclás connected every home with electricity, a road was built between Tierra de Chá and Coruña, and many houses had toilets installed inside. They were redirecting drinking water through pipes and had it running all the way to the town square. Still, there were no telephones. When they were laying the cables down by the side of the road, the whole village rose up to reject the possibility of a telephone booth. Why waste money on something nobody would use? Nearly every household got milking machines, but Dolores and Saladina didn't use theirs: they'd never betray Greta by hooking her up to some kind of breast pump.

Ever since Saladina applied the washes and rubs, the cow had been putting weight back on little by little; she kicked out again when the flies were bothering her, and she went back up the mountain, producing excellent milk—slightly acidic, but very good for making cheese that was the envy of all the neighbors.

Life slipped by like that for two or three weeks. Then one night, while they were eating dinner, the Winterlings heard bleating in the stable. One sister elbowed the other.

"Did you hear that?"

"I heard it."

"Was that bleating?"

"It was."

They sat there thinking. They had sold the sheep months ago. Even before the chickens flew off, caring for the cow was more than enough to keep them busy during the day. Someone made them a good offer, and they sold the three sheep and the newborn lamb. But what they had just heard was definitely bleating . . .

Dolores went to the bedroom and opened the trapdoor. Sitting down on her hind legs, Greta the cow was bleating at the stars with her mouth open, the way a sheep does.

She calmed down as soon as she had been milked, but by the next day she didn't have a single drop of milk left.

But it wasn't just Greta the cow. Meis's Widow had also started to act strangely, not to mention Uncle Rosendo.

The Widow asked her husband for bitter blackberries from the forest, curd, or cheese. Before making an omelet, she broke the egg and inspected it thoroughly to make sure there weren't two yolks. She did the same with chestnut shells, which sometimes come in pairs. She refused to take in the aroma of certain flowers or to touch the liver of a recently slaughtered pig. When she tied up the wagon, she avoided walking underneath the rope, for fear that it would get wrapped around "the child's" neck. But what child?

A child here, a child there.

Uncle Rosendo watched her bustling about the house, the way someone watches a fly flit about, listening to her anxiously as she prattled away. Then one day, he came home from school and found the Widow bent down in the paddock, as dirty as she was happy, eating handfuls of stones and soil like an animal. That's when he decided to ask her how she'd been feeling lately.

Meis's Widow lifted her head slowly. She looked like a little girl who'd been baking mud pies in the backyard.

"They say if you don't satisfy your cravings, they're born with blemishes on them," she told him.

Uncle Rosendo swallowed. For a good while now, ever since they saw all those gray butterflies in the sky, he'd noticed that his wife had stopped giving him hell. It wasn't as if she was especially *friendly*, but at least she no longer dedicated her time to making his life impossible, and that worried him. In the morning, when he left for school, she even said goodbye to him, and then when he got home, she had dinner prepared, and they sat chatting over coffee. She didn't talk about the past so much, or about her godforsaken *absence*, and one day, she even asked him to recite some poetry.

At one point, it crossed the teacher's mind that she might be pregnant, but two minutes later, he rejected the idea—his wife had had those kinds of fantasies before.

She had always had her fantasies, yes, and she had always insisted that until Rosendo gave her a child, she couldn't forget her dead husband.

But after a few days of watching her carefully, he thought it over again. The Widow's wrinkly old face had softened and was covered with a youthful patina of freckles. Isn't that what happened to women when they were expecting? Something bubbled and blossomed in his wife's insides, he was convinced of it, just like that fragrant plant she went to gather every day on the mountain and bring back in her wagon. And her stomach was beginning to swell . . .

In the tavern and by the communal oven, the rumor began to circulate that Uncle Rosendo had at last "fished out his tackle box," and they all praised his virility, asking him if his wife was lugging around any extra weight.

A few days later, Meis's Widow told them all the news they'd been waiting to hear.

Despite having suspected it, no one believed her, and the children even lifted her skirt, looking for a pillow. Then the Widow told her husband that she'd called for the doctor in Sanclás. He came after a few days and, after examining her, started slapping Uncle Rosendo on the back.

"Incredible but true," he said. "Sometimes surprises of this nature occur. How old are you anyway, Widow?"

"Fifty-two," she said proudly, as she zipped up her skirt.

"Incredible," said the doctor, shaking his head in disbelief. "Of course, strange things are known to happen in this village . . . "

Uncle Rosendo looked back and forth between the two of them. He couldn't give his opinion because he'd been left speechless. His wife was pregnant. He was going to be a father. A child! To tell the truth, he couldn't recall having relations with his wife, either recently or long ago, and yet . . .

"And my husband is sixty-three," said the Widow, settling that old question once and for all. "But he's always been quite well endowed."

If the doctor said it was so . . . This doctor was no quack. He'd studied for his medical degree in Santiago.

The Widow stopped going up the mountain to cut grass with her wagon. She got bigger and bigger, and there were no doubts about her pregnancy.

But Uncle Rosendo wasn't quite at ease. The more he thought about it, the stranger it all seemed. That's why he decided to go and see the priest. Surely he would have some explanation. Life was so stupid! He needed to know why his wife had gone sweet on him and was treating him so well all of a sudden. The doctor from Sanclás was right when he said strange things were happening in the village.

He found the priest in the living room of his house. When he heard someone ringing the doorbell, he quickly turned off the television and covered it with a dark cloth. The maid answered the door and informed him that it was the teacher, who wanted to speak with him. Don Manuel was delighted that a parishioner wished to seek his counsel.

The maid led Uncle Rosendo into the living room. The room was always cloaked in shadow and smelled of old things. There was an armchair, a table with a clock on it, damask curtains, two paintings depicting hunting scenes, and the covered television. On top of a wooden sideboard, there was a portrait of Don Manuel's mother. The old woman's gaze followed you all around the room.

Uncle Rosendo caught his breath.

"Father, the Virgin Mary . . . " he began.

"Yes?" responded the priest.

"The Virgin Mary . . . " stuttered Uncle Rosendo. "How does that work, exactly?"

"How does what work?"

"Well, you know—the virgin bit."

Don Manuel shifted in his chair.

"Get to the point, Rosendo."

Uncle Rosendo admitted that in fact he couldn't care less about the Virgin Mary. He explained what had happened to his wife and that he was worried by her change of attitude and the strange things that were going on in the village generally.

"It's not that I've noticed anything in particular," he added. "But I get this feeling that something is about to happen—many things, in fact."

Don Manuel listened to him with his eyes wide open.

"Me too," he said after a long while. "And I think . . . " He cleared his throat. "I'd venture to say that it has a lot to do with the arrival of the Winterlings in Tierra de Chá. They say one of them abandoned her husband . . . "

"*Abandoned?*"

"Call it what you will. And the other one makes strange lists with the names of everyone in the village."

"Our names?"

"Our names."

Rosendo agreed. He was convinced that after so long away, they hadn't come back without a reason. They had come back for revenge. He sat looking at the priest intently.

Don Manuel swallowed.

"Revenge, you say?"

"It's a real pity what you did to Don Reinaldo. He was my friend, you know. He didn't deserve that . . . Just because you couldn't last a few days without something to eat . . . "

The priest stood up and began pacing impatiently about the room. Then he sat down again.

"You're not entirely innocent either, Rosendo."

"But I had solid reasons," replied the teacher. "Don't you remember that every time they came for him and couldn't find him, they beat me up, just because I was the village teacher and because one time I said that poetry would save the world?"

The priest glanced over at the portrait of his mother.

"That's not the reason you did it, and you know that as well as I do," he said. "There's a reason you're here."

"That is the reason I did it," said Rosendo. "I have a clear conscience. If they hadn't carried him off, they would have killed me instead. That's the truth. It's no mystery."

Don Manuel's chin began to tremble. He pulled toward him a plate of churros that the maid had set down, but pushed it away.

"Behind gluttony lies fear," he said.

"No way," Rosendo rebuked him. "Stop making excuses. Gluttony doesn't hide fear, it's just gluttony—a sin, plain and simple."

The priest sighed with a certain sense of resignation and looked again at the portrait of his mother.

"It would be for the best if . . . if they didn't stay here."

"Who?"

"Those women."

"The Winterlings?"

They both looked at the floor in silence.

"They won't go," said the teacher heavily.

Then Don Manuel looked up and into Rosendo's eyes, clearing his voice.

"We'll see about that! I also believe that . . . things being the way they are, you shouldn't worry at all about your wife, in fact, quite the opposite," he said with a renewed voice. "If she says it's your child, then there's nothing to discuss. The birth of a child is always a blessing. And it wouldn't be the first time a woman's disposition changes when she is with child. When is she due?"

14

FROM THAT POINT ON, little by little, like a fog that finally lifts, Uncle Rosendo began to celebrate the news and think about the baby. With such a disaster by his side for so many years, the desire to be a father had been steadily eliminated from his mind. But now, seeing his wife's swelling belly and receiving the congratulations and compliments of the folks at the tavern, he was overcome by a humble domestic happiness. A child in those people's lives was like a ray of sunshine on a rainy day. Perhaps what had not been achieved in years and years of marriage could be achieved now with a child.

A child to whom he could read Rosalía de Castro's poetry.

He stopped drinking. In the evenings, instead of going to the tavern, he went to his shed: he was building a wooden crib. He cleaned out one of the rooms in the house and installed it there. He also collected toys that the children at school no longer wanted.

All this happiness went up in smoke one afternoon when the married couple were sitting in the living room. Throughout the morning, the Widow had been very taciturn, as if she wished to say something important but couldn't, and she kept staring out the window.

Finally, when Rosendo was about to finish off the room with a wooden rocking horse he'd rescued from the trash, he heard her voice.

"Listen, Rosen, are you busy?"

She had never called him by his name and certainly never by a pet name. Merely hearing that "Rosen" in his wife's mouth set him to trembling. So that his wife would think that he was busy, he didn't respond.

"You hear me, Rosendo? I want to talk with you."

At last, a tiny voice could be heard from the shadows of the room. "I'm listening . . . "

"Look, I know all this business about the child makes you happy . . . "

"Well, of course, woman! I can't stop thinking about it. We haven't exactly enjoyed our marriage, Mei . . . Meis's Widow. The years have gone by, and we've only become bigger strangers to each other. We haven't made much of a life together but . . . Look, I think that this baby will bring us together. The kid will get the best of each of us, you'll see, little Widow. You'll see how well it goes. Look at this beautiful little rocking horse I found yesterday, I'll fix it right up and—"

"That's what I wanted to talk to you about," she said.

Silence.

"About the rocking horse?"

"About the child."

There it was; the cat was out of the bag. Here came the moment Uncle Rosendo would have to hear that the child wasn't his. Well, of course, what was he thinking, that babies come along just like that, without marital relations? He didn't care whose it was. In the eyes of everyone in the village, he was the father, and he would continue to be.

He heard the Widow's voice.

"At first, I thought it was all different . . . But now I know that it's not. I wanted to tell you that nothing has changed between us and nothing ever will."

Uncle Rosendo didn't respond. He tried to decipher the meaning of the words he had just heard.

"I don't understand," he said.

"There's nothing to understand. Everything stays the same."

"Yes, except that there will be three of us now," said Rosendo.

"Four," pronounced the Widow.

Then Uncle Rosendo set about enlarging the rocking horse. He thought it would turn out even better than new.

15

MR. TENDERLOVE VISITED SALADINA from time to time, and the Winterlings were more and more convinced that it was he who had paid old Violeta to cure her with rubs and washes. His false-teeth business was booming; he had clients from all over, not just from the village but also from Sanclás and even farther away. Thanks to this, he'd bought himself a red SEAT 1400, and he spent the whole day driving about town, blaring the horn so that everyone would know he was the richest man in the village.

He hid his feminine side less and less often, and one day, he even dared to go into the tavern in a floral dress, with his hairy legs and high-heeled shoes.

By then, he'd been called "faggot" so many times that the word was hollow; it didn't bother him anymore.

That is, if it had ever bothered him in the first place.

As he had done for a very long time, in the evenings, after his last client had left, he went down the hallway and into the room with the pink walls to put on those colorful dresses and high heels and look at himself in the mirror.

For many years, after he searched for teeth, polished them, and tried to match them like puzzle pieces, after he leaned over his clients' putrid mouths to put the new teeth in, that moment of furtiveness had been his secret reward. Now things were different. Now the secret was meaningless, simply because everyone knew exactly what he did once he closed his office, everyone knew who he was . . .

One day, he stopped the car out the front of the sisters' house, and when he saw that Saladina was sitting in the sun in the orchard, he offered to take her for a drive. With the windows down, they passed by the fields and the communal oven, rattling over the gravel and waving to everyone by the lime trees. It was the first time in a long time that Saladina had gone out and enjoyed herself. She even let out a hearty laugh when Tenderlove stopped the car and turned around to grab something from the backseat: a bottle of local herb spirits.

"I don't need any anesthetics anymore," she said when she finally managed to stop laughing.

"So what?" he answered, offering her the bottle.

They each took a long swig. Then they sat there pensively, contemplating the lime trees.

"It doesn't taste the same, you know?" said the dental mechanic.

"I was just about to say the same thing. It's a bit tainted . . . " Saladina hiccupped twice. "It tastes like . . . it tastes like cork, or dirt, or—"

"Disappointment," interrupted Tenderlove. "Everything tastes like disappointment, especially those things we've been waiting a long time for."

They got back on the road. Saladina had gone quiet; she wasn't laughing and she'd stopped talking. But when they arrived at the church, she began to squirm in her seat, clutching at her pockets and searching around her, as if she wanted to get out.

"My God," she said. "I've left my list . . . "

Alarmed by the tone of her voice, Mr. Tenderlove stopped the car by the vestibule.

"Your list?" he asked, thinking that it might be an important list, with her medications or something of the sort.

Anxiety was written on Saladina's face, and her eyes glistened.

"My list."

"Your list of what?" asked Mr. Tenderlove. Suddenly, he thought it had been a bad idea to give spirits to a sick woman.

"The list of the Gothic kings."

"The mad kings?"

"That's the one. And my little scissors, too. My God! I must have left them in England!"

When they got home, Tenderlove told Dolores what had happened. She said that Saladina had many lists, and didn't think it was too important. Mr. Tenderlove held his tongue.

"Winterling," he said.

"What?"

"Weren't they waiting for you to make a movie somewhere? I heard something like that in the village."

"That's true."

"You should go, then."

Dolores looked at him, taken aback.

"My sister is sick. I can't go anywhere."

"That depends."

For a moment, Dolores and Tenderlove considered each other in silence.

"I already told you that everyone just wants to forget," he said.

"And they haven't forgotten yet? We burned the contracts of sale!"

Through the half-open door, Tenderlove cast an eye over the inside of the house.

"To forget, we need you two to leave . . . "

Dolores slammed the door in his face.

From then on, even if Saladina's stomach felt much better, she behaved strangely. She began to do things she had never done before, like leave pieces of knotted string all over the house, or refer to people that Dolores had never heard of, like "poor Dennis" or "stupid Margaret, who is as pure and virtuous as a cat."

It was true that she had many lists—she had spent half her life making them—but now anything and everything was susceptible to some new classification. There were cockroaches, bedbugs, and dead mosquitoes in the attic, and they were very different things, so she made a new list entitled "Insects with and without shells." To-do lists, thoughts. She classified and organized ideas, kinds of dogs, cars, and cleaning products, while she explained to her sister that not all men are fathers whereas, on the other hand, all fathers are men.

Lists here and there. There was nowhere left in the house to stick up another list.

In a box on the windowsill, next to a pot of geraniums, she kept a cricket she had found in the fields.

She would be doing one thing, and then the next minute she would jump up, spin around, and be overcome with uncontrollable despair.

She said that she had to leave.

"Where exactly do you have to go right now, woman?" her sister asked her as she sewed.

"To feed the cricket and water the geraniums."

Dolores put down her work and looked at her sister sadly.

To be stressed about feeding a cricket and watering some geraniums wasn't all that strange for her; after all, Saladina had always been a bit of a frantic woman. What worried her sister were the little slips of the mind. For example, she would sit down at the dinner table with a brassiere on her head, convinced it was a tiara. Hadn't Uncle Rosendo told them once that their grandfather did those sorts of things in his final days?

Although she had never been religious, Saladina set her mind on seeing Don Manuel for confession. And one day, in the middle of confession, she suddenly went silent, as if she had just remembered a mortal sin. She stuck her head through the curtain in the confession box and began talking, peppering the air with her onion and garlic breath.

"Father, you haven't seen a list around here, have you?"

Don Manuel knew of her passion for lists.

"No, woman, I suppose you're looking for the list of the Gothic kings? Did someone take it from you?"

"Yes, the commies robbed me. And they took some nail scissors, too."

"Don't you worry, I'm sure they'll turn up."

It was the end of October when Dolores knew without a shadow of a doubt that something was not right. She was making filloa pancakes in the kitchen when Saladina came over and lingered distractedly in the doorway, snapping the elastic of her underwear underneath her nightdress.

"Can I get you anything, Sala?" asked her sister.

"No, thank you." Saladina looked calm and happy. "I was just thinking. You remember the list of the kings? The one I had put away in the desk drawer?"

Dolores looked at her thoughtfully. In her face she saw something more than the wrinkles and the hooked nose. She saw vertiginous landscapes, a foggy morning, the back of a woman striding along a dock, nightfall, the intense sea, powerful and deep blue, colorful flags, and again the gray fog climbing over the houses. Rain. Birds and rain. Then, without knowing why, she thought of Albert Lewin's promise that she would be the lead actress in his next film. The director had told her that he didn't quite have it all figured out yet but intended it to be something exotic, filmed somewhere like Morocco, Syria, or Egypt, and that she would be perfect for the lead. Dolores realized that the letter would never arrive in a remote village like Tierra de Chá. She kept watching her sister, who was waiting for an answer, clicking her tongue against her teeth, like she always did when she was worked up.

"The list of the Gothic kings? How could I forget!" said Dolores finally. "And the nail scissors, too!"

"Do you think I left them in England?"

Dolores stopped stirring the filloa-pancake batter.

"No," she pronounced. "I don't think so."

But her answer left Saladina unmoved. After a moment, she asked again.

"You see, yesterday, when I was making up the bed in room 504, I put it on the tray so I wouldn't lose it. Sometimes, when I'm cleaning a bedroom—"

Dolores didn't let her finish.

"Saladina!" she exclaimed. "It's been over twenty years since you've set foot in England! It's been centuries since you cleaned rooms in that horrible hotel in Eastleigh where they made you work like a slave!"

Saladina stopped what she was doing. There was a mixture of surprise, worry, and terror in her eyes. She clutched at her stomach and had to sit down.

"I think . . . " continued Dolores, blowing a lock of hair out of her eyes and getting back to stirring the filloa batter, "I think that the commies stole it from you."

Suddenly, Saladina's contorted face relaxed.

"Yes," she said with relief. "No doubt it was the commies."

16

THE WHOLE VILLAGE was concerned, not just about Saladina's illness, but about everything that was going on.

For some time now, a hint of menace had been floating in the air, and you didn't need to be too clever to realize that soon it would precipitate something terrible. You could see it in the worn and worried faces of the villagers. You could smell it in the air and you could see it at dusk, when the sky was cut through with orange. You could sense it in muttered remarks, in contained smiles, in stifled laughter.

Often, moved by a morbid unease, they came by the house like lost animals, looking for answers. They popped their dirty faces in the window and asked after the patient, but Saladina was just an excuse: Dolores had the feeling that they all wanted them to leave the village, and, for that reason, at any time they might come along looking for a quarrel. Many times, she thought of packing her bags and leaving, disappearing just as easily as they had appeared (how nice it would be to take a boat and leave for America!), but Saladina wasn't in any shape for traveling.

And she would never leave her sister alone.

One day, Dolores went into the forest. Passing by Tristán's house, she was surprised to find him sitting in the doorway with his face in his hands and his elbows on his knees. She asked him what he was doing, just sitting around; didn't he have to feed one of his capons?

"Didn't you hear?" he answered. "The whole village saw it . . . "

"Hear about what?"

"My birds escaped, they flew off!"

Dolores glanced at the silent, empty house.

"Yes, we saw them," she said. "But now you've got plenty of time. Isn't that what you always wanted?"

"It's this horrible croaking . . . It's been going on all night!" he said.

"Croaking?"

"I have to make it stop, it's driving me crazy!" And he went back to sitting with his face in his hands.

Dolores continued on to Violeta da Cuqueira's cabin, hoping to ask her about some matters she was worried about. She found the old lady sitting in front of the fire. Wrapped up in a black cloak that went down to her toes, she looked like a big bald bird. The Winterling told her that although her sister's stomach was better, she was now sick in the head. Violeta didn't even look up and kept raking the coals of her fire.

"That's the thing with washes and rubs . . . "

The old lady explained that certain vapors from the rubs rose to the brain and sometimes had the unfortunate long-term side effect of the loss of reason. She also said that the rubs had only a limited effect and that soon the primitive illness would rear its ugly head again and that if Dolores liked, she could prepare a "liquor of future presence."

Dolores got up quickly and stalked over to the door before spinning around.

"Violeta," she said. "Do you remember, you once spoke to me about my dream of becoming an actress?"

Old Violeta da Cuqueira shut her eyes. She searched through the sea of memories in her mind.

"How . . . How did you know that?" continued the Winterling.

Da Cuqueira opened her eyes again.

"Why do you think your sister fell ill?"

Dolores again felt a chill crawl up her spine; she opened the door. She was just about to leave when she heard the old lady's voice.

"I hope you both get better, my girl."

That we *both* get better? The Winterling turned this over in her mind the whole way home.

Once she got home, she climbed the stairs to see Saladina and was surprised to hear the voice of the priest. Lately, Don Manuel had been coming with his holy oils—just like he had with the old lady from Bocelo—to bring solace to Saladina. This time, seeing that the sister was not there, he made the bold move of going up alone to the bedroom. Through the open door, Dolores listened to their conversation. The priest asked Saladina if she had found her list of Gothic kings, to which Saladina replied, with a distracted and insolent manner, that she had no idea what list he was talking about.

"The one the commies stole from you."

Saladina looked at him in confusion.

"You know what, Woolly Caterpillar?" she said to him, in English, as if she had never even heard of this story about the list of Gothic kings.

"What did you say, my daughter? You know my English is not what it might be . . . "

"I just remembered something that might interest you . . . A tiny detail about my sister, Woolly."

"Yes?"

On the other side of the doorway, Dolores went red. From the sound of her voice, Saladina seemed perfectly lucid.

"You know how my sister has this big idea in her head that she wants to become an actress?"

"I've heard something like that, yes. She's quite pretty."

"And you know that she was married, right?"

"I've also heard something about that . . . "

Saladina clicked her tongue.

"Do you know what happened to her husband?"

The priest leaned in close to hear better.

"No, what?"

Saladina smiled maliciously.

Suddenly, Don Manuel jumped up and began shouting.

"She killed him! His body is in the stable, isn't it? I always knew it! We all knew it! Someone saw you getting it down from the covered wagon that day you arrived in Tierra de Chá . . . "

Dolores's heart was in her mouth. She pushed the door open and burst in.

"Shut up!"

The priest jumped in fright when he saw her. Saladina, however, carried on as if nothing had happened.

"And so her husband Tomás, the fisherman of octopus and pout whiting . . . "

"Shut up!" Dolores screeched again.

Saladina looked at her. Suddenly, she seemed to have taken in her presence, and she lowered her head.

"Yes, shut up," she mumbled.

"Put up and shut up!" they shouted in unison.

The priest didn't know how to react. On the one hand, he wanted to keep asking questions, but, on the other hand, Dolores was already looking at him murderously.

"No!" he heard. Saladina had stood up and was looking at her sister intensely. "Enough shutting up. We've kept quiet long enough. Leave us, Dolores. I need to talk to the priest *alone*."

For the first time in a long time, Saladina scolded her sister. So that's what the calm was all about. Dolores realized that her sister's pretending for all these previous days was nothing more than a vile betrayal. She should never have told her about Tossa de Mar.

With the priest looking on inquisitively, she had no other option but to go out of the room and leave them alone.

She thought about putting an ear to the closed door to hear what they were talking about, but in the end she didn't do it.

She went down to the kitchen and sat down to wait.

17

OUR LITTLE SECRET.

Or perhaps now she should say, *her* little secret.

Sitting in the kitchen, waiting anxiously for the priest to come out of the bedroom, the Winterling couldn't help but remember that tragic day in 1948.

Not long after her wedding, Dolores had left her Tomás under the pretense of having to care for her sister. She had already been in Coruña with Saladina for several weeks, sewing in the workshop. The dry, sunny season arrived, but the fog of worry never left her face.

"Do you remember what our grandfather used to say about how a bad thought or an unfulfilled desire always ends up festering until it becomes an illness?" said Saladina one day.

Dolores nodded with tears in her eyes.

"Well, I don't want you crying or worrying over that fisherman any longer," she continued. "Tell me what I need to know. I won't say anything, and everything will go back to how it used to be."

And so Dolores had no other option but to tell her sister everything. In a soft voice, without anger or sadness, she told her about how little affection she had received from her husband in the time they had been together, how badly he treated her, how he insulted her. One day, he found a hair in his coffee and slapped her. Another day, he told her she was worthless and locked her in the basement.

By God, he snored. And he stank, not of farts, but of fish. Dolores told Saladina about his threat to come and find her and kill her.

"I don't want to hate him, Sala, but I've got so much pain in my heart—"

"Don't get carried away," Saladina interrupted. "Hatred doesn't come from the heart, it's made in the belly."

They spent the whole night reflecting. By dawn, the plan was ready. The Winterlings took the first bus in the morning to Ribeira.

When Tomás saw the two sisters come in together—tall, gangly, and nervous, locking the door behind them—he began to tremble.

But they calmed him down. He had nothing to be afraid of, they told him. One Winterling took his shoes off and sat him down. The other one hurried off to the kitchen to prepare something to eat. *Tomás, Little Tomás, we've come to look after you.*

In the blink of an eye, they'd tidied the whole house. The room they found themselves in was clean and homely, the curtains drawn, the floor swept. It smelled good.

Very good.

And so Tomás, seeing the smiling and conciliatory gestures of the sisters, calmed down and began to feel at ease. Really, he thought, it's just my wife and my sister-in-law . . .

"Are you tired?" they asked.

"Exhausted," he replied.

One Winterling rushed off to get his slippers, and the other fetched a bottle of whiskey and a glass and served him.

"We'll make dinner for you, Tomás. What have you got in the house to eat?"

"Octopus," he said, a bit confused. "But it's no good, it hasn't been cured."

"It's a shame that a man like you should have to go out fishing so early. Tomorrow, you'll rest like a king. Have some whiskey. What did you say you had for dinner?"

"Octopus," answered the other Winterling for him. "He said that there's some octopus in the basement for dinner. It hasn't been cured, but that doesn't matter, we'll cure it ourselves. What else would an octopus fisherman have in his cupboards?"

That was when Dolores got up and walked across the room. She felt nothing.

Slowly, she went down the stairs and into the basement. What lay down there below in the basement had always been alluring. Down there was the kingdom of shadows, but also all the cast-off odds and ends, the hidden treasures. Down there were all the household knickknacks, little bits and bobs, hooks, lines, nylon, old tackle boxes, the remains of some whale-like creature, the uncured octopus. Down there was the most remote, the most dust-covered stuff: there lay everything rotted by brine and dampness, the forgotten and the feared things, the things that should remain hidden. There lay the most opaque shadows, and while Dolores searched for the light switch that day, she thought that sooner or later, we all go toward them.

She found the octopus on a table. She picked it up and went back up the stairs.

When she arrived upstairs, she saw Saladina's smiling face as she sat next to Tomás.

"You have to cure the octopus," he said as he stared at the ground. "It's all hard, you can't eat it like that."

"Yes," said Dolores with a dry voice. "Turn around."

"Turn around?" he said. "What for?"

Dolores had gone quiet. She trembled next to him.

"It's a surprise," said Saladina.

Tomás turned around. No one had ever been so attentive to him.

Then Dolores smacked him over the head with the octopus so hard that he stumbled around and collapsed onto the floor.

"The octopus is cured," said Saladina, seeing how the slimy legs of the octopus hung down by her sister's knees.

"Yes," said Dolores, still out of breath, dropping it to the ground. "And my husband is dead."

The wait was dragging on forever. How long had they been talking in the bedroom? Five minutes? Three hours? Hearing the door, Dolores got up quickly. Don Manuel came down the stairs heavily. His face gave away nothing, but Dolores thought that in his eyes danced a quiet but definite victory.

The priest limited himself to saying only that Saladina had made her peace with the Lord.

18

UNHINGED, SALADINA WANDERED about the house all day. She was always watering the geraniums and feeding her cricket, whom she had affectionately begun calling Adolf Hitler. She babbled in English about "stupid Margaret, who is as pure and virtuous as a cat" and "poor little Dennis." "What can we do, Dolores, to make him feel better?"

In the mornings, they sat down to eat breakfast together. But Saladina, who was immersed in the production of her interminable lists, barely even spoke.

"Sala, do you remember much about our grandfather?" Dolores asked her one day.

Saladina was absorbed in her list, her tongue hanging out as she wrote.

"Oh yes. I remember Grandfather."

"What was he like?"

"Grandfather? Well . . . He was a delight."

Dolores sat in silence as her sister crossed out and added new names to her list.

"And do you know who I am?"

"You're a delight as well," said Saladina, not looking up from her list.

"Yes . . . But who am I?"

"Well . . . you . . . " Saladina looked up at her sister with surprise. "You're . . . you're my sister."

"Yes," said Dolores. "But what's my name?"

"How would I know?" exclaimed Saladina, and went back to completing her list.

Dolores sat there looking at her. For just a moment, while she contemplated the tangled hair covering her sister's face, her fragile hand filling up the piece of paper with useless classifications, the hint of an idea flashed across her mind. *If Saladina were dead . . . nobody would find out about* our little secret, *and then nobody could stop me from fulfilling my destiny.* Two seconds later, the terrible weight of regret came over her. The same weight she had known for years. How could she have such thoughts when her sister was ill, very ill? How could she think of leaving so selfishly when Saladina needed her more than ever? And then, she had confessed to the priest. What could she have told him? Thinking about that drove her mad. She was sure that the priest knew everything and that he was just waiting for the right moment to reveal it.

She brushed the hair out of her sister's eyes and kissed her forehead.

"Would you like me to tell you a story?" she asked. Saladina looked up from her list.

"Yes, a story."

"Once upon a time, there was a very bad wolf who lived in the forest. One stormy night—"

"No, not that story."

"I've told you the one about the Taragoña Express about a thousand times. Why don't you let me tell you the one about the wolf who gets struck by lightning?"

"No, not that story."

Dolores sighed.

"Once upon a time, there was a man who was all skin and bones, with a long scraggly beard just like Jesus Christ, who . . . "

Then Dolores thought that no matter what happened in her life, she'd never become an actress.

Doing that would be worse than betraying Saladina. It would kill her.

And so life went on: care, patience, and warm embraces. Soon, visitors began arriving.

One afternoon, when Dolores had gone off to the tavern, Saladina sat on the bench by the door to wait for her. She heard footsteps on the road and got up to receive her sister with a hug. She took a few steps forward, intending to surprise her by meeting her at the end of the road, but instead she stood there staring. Dolores wasn't coming back alone. She and her companion, who was none other than Albert Lewin, the director of *Pandora and the Flying Dutchman*, stopped a few yards from the house and started kissing. Saladina went upstairs quickly and hid under the covers. Dolores came up twenty minutes later and kissed her on the forehead.

"How are you, Sala?"

"I'm fine."

Saladina felt strange.

The next time, Saladina opened the door to find Dolores tangled in the sheets with Mr. Tenderlove, who smiled at her over her shoulder.

First thing in the morning, her hair a mess, she told her sister all this, over and over again in English.

"I had visitors last night, Dolores," she also said. "Lots of people walking around my bedroom . . . You were there, too. What were you doing in my bedroom?" she added in a serious tone.

She forgot how to sew.

She let Adolf the cricket die, and the geraniums dried out.

She forgot how to write and no longer made lists.

She prayed. She prayed endlessly and ate omelets with cheese.

Don Manuel, the priest, came to see her every day. He brought the sacraments and prepared last rites for her.

She was a frail thing. Her skin had shriveled up; she was barely a bag of bones.

Violeta da Cuqueira was right: the illness had come back with a vengeance.

She died a few hours after the cow. Greta, too, had gone from bad to worse. Ever since the day she had woken up bleating like a sheep, she had barely eaten and spent most of the day sleeping. One night, Dolores was surprised that she couldn't hear shuffling and mooing in the stable. With a terrible premonition, she went down to the stable. Greta had keeled over on her side, lying dead on the bed of gorse.

Dolores crouched down and sat there for a while, breathing in Greta's scent. She felt her warmth and the thrumming of flies around her. She went upstairs for a sheet and some cord, then wrapped her up completely and tied her off. She cleared the gorse away from one side of the stable and, with the pick and the shovel, dug until she had a decent-sized hole. She covered her with earth and branches.

When she finished, she looked out the window. The world at dawn revealed itself to her: the burbling of the river, distant echoes from the forest, sharp and terrifying shrieks from little creatures. She doubled over, trying to contain her sobbing.

She burst into tears.

She cried for the cow, but most of all she cried for what she knew was lost from that moment on. She cried for Saladina making

fig jam in the kitchen. She cried for the sound of her teeth clicking in the mornings, for the smell of her hot urine. She cried for
the ferocious odor of her loins. She cried for the mashed banana
sandwiches that they used to eat in England and for the stench of
stale popcorn in the cinemas. She cried for the roosting chickens
and for the sound of the cowbell as they went up the mountain.
She cried for the yellow resplendence of the gorse flower. She
cried for the film she would never star in, for the sound of Mr.
Tenderlove's red car wending through the back roads. She cried
for Tierra de Chá.

She cried for life.

She cried for her.

Finally, she wiped away her tears with her apron, went to the
kitchen, and made breakfast for her sister before taking it up. She
found her sitting up in bed, wearing those thick glasses she used
for sewing. She put water in a bowl and left it on her sister's lap so
that she could wash her hands. She dropped in a bar of soap and left
her hands in the bowl, too. For a while, their hands intertwined in
the soapy water, seeking each other out like fish, brushing against
each other.

"Are they my fingers or yours?" said one Winterling.

"What difference does it make?" answered the other, after some
thought.

They both started laughing.

Once the bowl had been cleared away, Saladina drank her cup of
anise and ate a bit of cheese omelet, but she didn't have the strength
for much more.

"Did Greta . . .?" she asked.

"Yes," answered Dolores.

Saladina took off her glasses and sat watching the countryside from the window. The wind shook the cornstalks ferociously. From time to time, it carried the echoes of church bells.

"No one will ever know that her real name is Teixa," said one sister.

"Or that we stole her," said the other one. "So many secrets! Do you remember how scared we were that someone would recognize her?"

Silence fell over them again.

Outside, a crow croaked.

"You never told me the reason for all that running," said Saladina after a time.

"Greta's running?" asked her sister, puzzled.

"No, the Taragoña Express," she answered.

Dolores the Winterling sat thinking about it. So many years telling that same story, and she herself had never stopped to think why that man ran about day and night.

"It doesn't matter," said her sister. "I don't even want to know anymore. We've had some good times together, haven't we, Dolores?"

"We sure have."

"We had fun, didn't we?"

"I think so . . . "

Then Saladina made a gesture for her sister to come close and whispered a single lucid sentence in her ear, ten words that Dolores would never forget and that, in truth, she never knew quite how to interpret: "You can go to Hollywood now to become an actress."

Dolores began to hiccup.

"Are you giving me your blessing? Really? And what about our little secret? What about my little secret? Does the priest know? What did you tell him? I have to know!"

But Saladina went silent; she fell into a deep and peaceful sleep, and shortly thereafter, she passed away.

Dolores watched over the body all night. Then she tried to sleep a little.

She felt terribly relieved.

THE NEXT MORNING, after sleeping for a couple of hours, Dolores went down to the kitchen. Her sister lay still on the stretcher she had prepared for her.

"Sala, can you hear me, Sala?"

Saladina's mute presence filled the room.

Dolores went silent, then began talking excitedly.

"I know I need to get a move on . . . But I'm confused . . . It's difficult, you know? We always did everything together . . . "

She waited again in silence.

"Don't you worry, I'll take off that nightdress and put something pretty on you. But let me just ask you one thing . . . " Her pulse quickened, she stopped and then started again with a feeble groan. "Do you still think I should go, Sala? I don't want to do anything you don't approve of, now that . . . "

Dolores spent the whole morning thinking about how she would arrange for her sister's burial. At around midday, she wanted to move the body, but it had begun to stiffen and was difficult to move. She grew more and more confused and weary. Then she heard a knock at the door.

It was the priest, accompanied by nearly the whole village. When they saw him going past with his bag of holy oils, once again in the direction of the Winterlings' house, the villagers couldn't help but follow. Along the way, others joined them.

When she opened the door, Dolores felt herself give in to

happiness, feeling the most absolute gratitude. Seeing all those people there, she felt she had been mistaken. Deep down, they were good people after all: they were prepared to help out and bring comfort in difficult times. And so while she let them in, she explained in a trembling voice that she needed help to go to Sanclás to buy a . . . then she'd have to come back and . . .

"My sister is dead," she announced at last.

There was a general silence. Don Manuel crossed himself.

"Jesus Christ!" said Meis's Widow, covering her mouth with her hand.

They came into the house and filed slowly by the body. Some of them kissed her knees and feet.

"She looks sad," said Aunty Esteba, screwing up her nose.

"And thinner," added Meis's Widow. She still had her hand over her mouth, as if that way she might avoid throwing up.

"What a shame!" said the *gaitero*, the local bagpiper from Sanclás, who by chance was in town that morning. "All those new teeth and barely any time to use them."

"Considering how expensive they are!" said Tristán. "I was thinking of getting some myself, and look . . . What's the point? We all end up like her."

They stood silently while the priest prayed in Latin. Dolores noticed then that three or four women were whispering to one another. They looked over at the priest before dashing out toward the shed. Don Manuel stopped praying for a few seconds. Moments later, the women came back with a pick and a shovel and went down to the stable.

"Where are you going with those? Stop that!" he screeched, wiping beads of sweat off his forehead. "I'm telling you, you should wait for the Civil Guard."

The women stopped dead in front of the stable door. They turned around and stood next to Dolores, the stretcher with Saladina on it and the group of villagers surrounding them. But they were impatient and didn't put down the pick or the shovels.

"My sister is going rigid," said the Winterling. "We have to shroud her and put her in the coffin right away. I haven't got . . . I haven't got a coffin yet."

The priest made no response and kept praying, his fingers entwined in his lap, visibly excited. The women, who hadn't stopped whispering and fidgeting among themselves, decided to ignore the priest's instructions and head into the stable. For a good while, you could hear them scratching away in the gorse: "Have a look here," said one; "Move that branch, what a stink," said another, and then more moving of branches and crunching of dry leaves; "Phwoah, it has to be here, keep digging, yes, dig away. . . "; "But didn't he say it was in the stable?"; "Yes, here, it must be around here. Look, here the earth has been turned over . . . "

From time to time, Don Manuel opened his eyes, listened in, then let out a sigh, shaking his head. "I told them it would be better to wait for the Civil Guard to begin the search," he whispered to himself. The other men also listened to the hubbub with interest.

And then everything went silent.

Horribly silent.

The group of women marched out, leaving the pick and the shovels abandoned on the ground. They looked like they'd just seen a ghost; they pushed each other in their rush to get out. Meanwhile, the priest began to make way between them.

*

"What's going on?" he yelled. "There's nothing there! What did you see? Was it *him*? Tell me something, for the love of God! I told you you should have waited for the Civil Guard!" He addressed himself to Dolores. "But your sister told me he wasn't here!"

"This has nothing to do with my sister," she said calmly.

"She told me what she had done . . . "

"Then she lied to you."

The priest wiped the sweat from his forehead again. He began to stutter.

"But, dear woman . . . How could you?"

"And what would you have done in my place?"

Those who had been waiting in the living room began to grow impatient. The circle of people around Saladina's stretcher melted away. The Widow said that it wasn't as if she didn't want to help, God no, but she had never liked being around the dead. She was followed out by Uncle Rosendo, who shrugged as he excused himself: What was he supposed to do? Where there's a captain, a sailor gives no orders. Aunty Esteba suddenly remembered that she had left bread baking in the oven, and went off, saying that she'd be back later. She was the one who always dressed the departed, and she had no problem helping out. Only the priest, Tristán, the bagpiper from Sanclás, and two other villagers remained.

The two villagers and the bagpiper were of the opinion that a woman who had lost her sister would need solitude and time to reflect and that it would be best if they left. Tristán looked at his watch and left also. At the door, he turned around and confusedly muttered something about his birds squawking. Then the priest, who for some time now had had one foot out of the door, decided that the best thing would be to call Mr. Tenderlove, who could take Dolores in his car to Sanclás to buy a coffin. And so he set off to find him.

Dolores was alone once more. Lying on the stretcher, her sister had acquired an ashen tinge. She was now so stiff that it would be impossible to dress her. *Just as Saladina had told me, months ago, even before she fell ill*, thought Dolores sadly.

Hours later, as it began to grow dark, the Winterling set out to find Tenderlove at his house. She was walking gravely, all erect and lonesome, when she saw the priest running at full speed in the opposite direction. Don Manuel looked up at her for a second, then looked away again. Dolores noticed that the cuffs of his cassock had mud and burrs from the shortcuts he had taken.

She went back up the main street, up the spine of the fish, as it were. The village was empty; the emptiness seemed somehow to fill everything. Where was everyone? Where were the animals? She crossed paths with a dirty-blonde girl with blue eyes who had a wooden pail on her head and scuttled off immediately. Then she passed in front of the school. At that moment, Uncle Rosendo came out, clipping one of the kids over the ear. Seeing the Winterling pass by, he stood still. The children began to whisper among themselves.

"I didn't say anything before because there were people around, but I think I'm going to follow your advice, Rosendo," said Dolores.

Uncle Rosendo kicked a small child out of the way and shuffled over.

"My advice?"

"I'm going to face up to my moment of truth," she replied.

The Winterling was expecting an effusive reaction from Uncle Rosendo, some kind of discourse on fear and the mechanics of the moment, but it never came.

"Ah," was his only response. "Perhaps . . . "

But Uncle Rosendo couldn't go on. Meis's Widow was already there, pulling at his arm and telling him to go inside.

Dolores found Mr. Tenderlove in his workshop. With a degree of spite, she asked him if the priest had informed him of her sister's passing.

"He . . . He told me," said Tenderlove, somewhat embarrassed. "It's just that I'm in the middle of polishing, I've got a client from Coruña . . . How about that, Coruña! He's coming first thing in the morning, and I haven't been able to get away."

Dolores stood waiting. She wasn't entirely sure she'd understood about the polishing. At last the dental mechanic put down what he was doing, and, putting his shirt back on to go out, he said that he had no problems helping out, that for Saladina he would give his life, and even his teeth.

They went to Sanclás in the SEAT 1400, bought a coffin, and took it back home. Once he was inside, Tenderlove didn't seem moved by Saladina's body. He looked at her very calmly, as if she'd been dead all her life.

"One day, the priest came into the tavern all excited and told us all that Saladina had just confessed to killing your husband, *all by herself*, because of jealousy, but that the body wasn't here . . . " said Tenderlove after a while.

Dolores pretended not to hear.

"First, we need to get a clean dress on her," she said.

She went up to the bedroom and took out several dresses and Saladina's red silk stockings. These were the clothes they'd brought all the way from England, clothes they'd barely worn in the village. She came back down and put it all out on the table. Tenderlove recognized the stockings.

"Sweet Mother of Mary! It's the red stockings made from the parachutes of the German enemy! What I wouldn't give for a pair like that . . . They even match my car!" He let out a chortle, but,

seeing Dolores's severe disposition, he stopped laughing and continued talking. "But none of us believed him . . . the priest, that is.
The womenfolk were sure the body of that Tomás, your Tomás, was
in the stable, because one time Meis's Widow said she saw a hand
rising out of the gorse branches. And also, someone saw you getting
him down off the wagon when you arrived in Tierra de Chá . . . "

"I think I'll put this dress on her," said Dolores, again speaking as
if she couldn't hear a word of his macabre speech. "Give me a hand,
please, lift up her feet."

Tenderlove did as he was told, but he couldn't keep his eyes off
the stockings. He was holding up her feet when Saladina's mouth
popped open. Her new teeth shone whiter and brighter than ever.
The dental mechanic stopped in his tracks and stared at them.
Dolores understood at once.

"Get of here, you tooth-pulling quack! Out of my house!"

Tenderlove took a step back.

"I'm sick of being treated like a monster," he boomed. "Pulling
out teeth from dead people's mouths is nothing compared to pulling
out brains and killing husbands . . . No one asked you to come back.
We were just fine here. Don't you realize now that both of you need
to get away . . . that *you* need to go, at all costs? I can't even explain
it to you! You should never have come back!"

Dolores grabbed the broom and raised it in front of the dental
mechanic. But suddenly she stopped.

"Explain yourself! Can someone explain this to me? Why do you
need me to leave? And what the hell happened to my grandfather
on that October night in 1936?"

But Tenderlove wouldn't say a word more. He closed the door
and walked off, lightly swaying, down the main road.

*

228

The Winterling shook with fury as she dressed her sister. "Turn over, Sala, turn over," she said. "Give me your hand, Sala, I'm going to dress you, help you get dressed." When at last she had her ready, she plaited her hair and put lipstick on her. "There we are!"

With great difficulty, she managed to get her into the box.

1936 . . .

As he walked down the road, Mr. Tenderlove saw the images of that frosty October night file past in his mind.

The priest had told him that Don Reinaldo was hiding in the church. In the vestry there was a trapdoor, and the Winterlings' grandfather had spent months down there, stashed away next to the supplies he sent up every day to be shared out.

After barely two days, the whole town was gathering there. From the trapdoor, they asked for the return of the contracts of sale for their brains, saying that they didn't want to end up like Esperanza and Old Lady Resurrección. It was this, and not the food, that truly had everyone worried. Don Reinaldo repeated that if that was what they wanted, then they needed to give him back the money.

There were insults and arguments.

Two days later, the Civil Guard arrived at the church. Someone had informed them that the Bolshevik doctor, friend to the poets, was hidden inside somewhere. At gunpoint, they rounded up the whole village. They tried to force the priest to reveal the secret hiding place in the vestry, but he refused; he said he'd never be an informer like Tenderlove.

Then the guards started shouting and asking the others to collaborate.

Everyone was there, sitting among the pews: the baker's wife; the shoemaker; Uncle Rosendo, who hung his head; Meis's Widow, who trembled slightly; Tristán, who was giggling nervously . . .

Finally, the cornered priest said that it wasn't up to him to decide if they'd give up Don Reinaldo. He said that everyone else in the pews knew exactly where that man was hiding, too.

One by one, the guards asked around. First Uncle Rosendo said that Don Reinaldo was close, very close . . . Then Meis's Widow said that that was true, he was somewhere in the vestry. The guards inspected the vestry, and without finding anything, they continued their interrogation. Two old ladies began crying, and Tristán commented, as if it were nothing, that there was a trapdoor in the vestry. Aunty Esteba told them exactly where it was. It was the priest who, at last, told them how to open it, because there was a bit of a trick to it.

It was raining, and the bats flew in circles through the air.

Dolores went out of the house and walked toward the shed. She got out the shovel and began to dig next to the fig tree. When she had a nice big hole, she dragged her sister's coffin out of the house. She put it in the hole and covered it with dirt. Then she went back inside. With determination, she picked up one of the Singer sewing machines and went upstairs. She dragged it over to the window. She was shaking. "Of course we had some good times," she said to herself. And then she hurled it out.

The machine bounced off one of the branches of the fig tree and shattered on the ground.

She went back downstairs, and then came up again with the second Singer. She hurled it out the window as well.

Throwing the machines away like that seemed so beautiful to her.

*

Two hours later, Tenderlove's car came around the corner, followed by a group of people.

Those inside got out. At the head of the party was the priest, with a mean glint in his eye. Behind him came Tenderlove, Tristán, and some of the women. Uncle Rosendo cowered behind the Widow's swollen belly.

The rain kept falling. They opened their umbrellas and positioned themselves in a circle around the front door. Black crows cut through the gray day. They saw the remains of the sewing machines, the spools broken, the wheel in pieces. The earth turned over next to the fig tree.

A pair of Civil Guards also came with the group, and they stopped in front of the house and knocked on the door. They yelled that they had come to search the stable, due to some neighbors locating a suspicious cadaver . . . that had been wrapped in a sheet and tied with cord.

But no one responded. The Winterling was no longer there.

Nobody saw her slip off through the cornfields.

Perhaps along the road that leads to Portugal.

AUTHOR'S ACKNOWLEDGMENTS

I would like to thank Luciana Gil, Elisabeth Sánchez-Andrade, Patricia Sánchez, and especially Nuria Barrios for their generous and patient critiques.

I would also like to thank my aunts, especially María Paz, who inherited their passion for storytelling from my grandmother, for their patience in bringing all these stories and characters back to life. And thanks also to my mother Bárbara, who accompanied me through the lands of Galicia in search of family memories.

ABOUT THE AUTHOR AND TRANSLATOR

CRISTINA SÁNCHEZ-ANDRADE (Santiago de Compostela, 1968) has degrees in Law and Mass Media. She is a writer and translator, and she collaborates in various Spanish newspapers and literary magazines as a critic and book reviewer. She is also the coordinator of several narrative workshops. She is the author of the novels *Las lagartijas huelen a hierba* (Lengua de Trapo, 1999), *Bueyes y rosas dormían* (Siruela, 2001), *Ya no pisa la tierra tu rey* (Anagrama, Premio Sor Juana Inés de la Cruz, 2004), *Alas* (Trama Editorial, 2005), *Coco* (2007), *Los escarpines de Kristina de Noruega* (Roca Editorial, 2011, finalist to Premio Espartaco de Novela Histórica), *El libro de Julieta* (Grijalbo, 2011), and *Las Inviernas* (*The Winterlings*, Anagrama, 2014). Her work has been translated into English, Portuguese, Italian, Polish and Russian.

SAMUEL RUTTER is a writer and translator from Melbourne, Australia. A recipient of a PEN Translates award in 2015, he currently resides in Nashville, where he attends the MFA program at Vanderbilt University.

RESTLESS BOOKS is an independent publisher for readers and writers in search of new destinations, experiences, and perspectives. From Asia to the Americas, from Tehran to Tel Aviv, we deliver stories of discovery, adventure, dislocation, and transformation.

Our readers are passionate about other cultures and other languages. Restless is committed to bringing out the best of international literature—fiction, journalism, memoirs, poetry, travel writing, illustrated books, and more—that reflects the restlessness of our multiform lives.

Visit us at www.restlessbooks.com.